Whitewater VI

Whitewater VI

Douglas McBriarty

Walker and Company
New York

First published in the United States of America in 1987 by the Walker Publishing Company, Inc.

Published simultaneously in Canada
by Thomas Markham & Son
Canada, Limited, Markham, Ontario

Library of Congress Cataloging-in-Publication Data

McBriarty, Douglas, 1918–
Whitewater VI.
I. Title. II. Title: Whitewater six.
PS3563.C3336W4 1987 813'.54 87-14740
ISBN 0-8027-5686-7

Printed in the United States of America

10 9 8 7 6 5 4 3 2 1

This book is dedicated to
Kathleen, my wife.

Whitewater VI

Prologue

IT IS ONE of the most wild and scenic rivers in America. The United States government by Act of Congress proclaimed this to be so in 1974 and for many years back had been acquiring all the land on both sides of the river to keep it that way. No towns, no settlements, no clusters of summer cottages: just three bridges, two fords, three or four places to put in or take out, and a few lonesome trails for hiking. For the rest of the forty-two miles it's just the river, the rocks, the woods, and the wilds.

From high peaks and hidden valleys, or coves as they are called way up in the Smokies, to where it finally flows into a long, slender lake, it drops almost four thousand feet, or four feet in every hundred. But it changes pace. After flowing through wooded fields and wide, serene pools, it can suddenly buckle and go rolling and hurtling down rocky ravines with sheer drops of six or eight feet. Like a wet, writhing roller coaster, it can be very thrilling, very beautiful, and very dangerous. These danger spots are located on the government charts and are classified from I to VI according to the risk involved. VI is described on these charts as "Ultimate limit of navigability, danger of loss of life." Two spots on the river are designated as Whitewater VI; one is the Eye of the Needle, and the other is Bull Sluice.

Why run the river? Some say simply because it's

there. But that is not even a half-truth. The natural beauty draws most people. For others it's the challenge and adventure. The brush with death that tells them they are unafraid, and once again makes them whole and strong.

They say that twenty-one people have been killed on the river. No one knows for sure. If, however, that figure is correct, this is the story of the twenty-third.

1

Bateman's Ford

JAYNES LOVED TO be on the river before dawn. He shoved the bow off a small, brown sand spit and with two easy strokes backed into the slack water. Then, with a wide sweep of the paddle, he brought the bow of the canoe around to catch the current. He adjusted his knee pads, took a strong, full stroke, and was off in the whitewater.

The Devil's Chimney loomed up out of the darkness, and Jaynes hung close enough to reach out and touch the jutting pillar of rock as he swept by. Then he let the rushing water take him over the first drop into the pool below.

He drifted now, trailing the paddle and letting the fog of the river and the unseen woods on both sides close in on him until he was a part of it. The fiery devils of the corporate world dropped their pitchforks and fled, leaving him whole and strong again in the stillness and solitude of his river.

Finally, he lifted the paddle, reached forward to stroke, and stopped in midair. An alien sound came through the fog. He let the paddle come down slowly and silently into the water and rest next to the gunwale. There it was again! A car engine, a little louder, now, over the sound of the water. He followed it, moving his head slowly, and then it was gone. He waited. Someone else at the launch site. Someone else running the river before dawn. Someone behind him.

He was annoyed more than anything else. It was to have been just him and the river. Now it was him and the river and someone behind him. No one else ever ran the river before dawn. There was never a time when he hadn't been alone. Unless you knew that river like the back of your hand, you never started out at daybreak.

He listened, hoping for the sound of the engine again. Perhaps they were just looking. Maybe it was just a ranger checking the area. Once he thought he heard voices, but the sound of the water drowned them out.

Strange, in a way. First it was the helmet. He knew he had put it in the corner of the truck after the last trip. It was always there. Last week, the week before, and the week before that. This morning, no helmet. Now it was someone behind him. That, too, was a first.

His eyes searched the fog on both sides, and he tilted his head to listen as he looked behind him. He felt sure he was not alone in the cocoon of heavy, leaden fog and black water.

He was drifting too far to the left, and those knee pads were loose again. Jaynes pulled on them and smiled a little to himself. Loose knee pads, an early morning visitor, and no helmet. He didn't like the helmet anyway. It kept him from hearing the telltale changes in the sound of the water. He dug in and swung the canoe towards the right bank. That was the clear entry to the next rapids.

The water reading at the launch site, Bateman's Ford, had been 3.5 feet. High water. This would give him a fast trip. Eleven miles from Bateman's Ford to his take out. He'd be on the river for two hours and thirty, maybe forty, minutes.

He pulled further to the right. Most of the whitewater in Section III was fairly tame all the way down to the sluice. Bull Sluice was something else. But that was almost an hour away. He swung around and slipped into the rapids exactly as he had planned.

2

The Pickup

In the morning's first light, a heavy mist hangs over the mountains and the river and fills the narrow valley with gray, cottony cloud. It makes dark shapes out of the tall pines on each side and filters the soft light from above to a pitch blackness below. Beneath this mantle of mist and fog the whitewater runs full and strong.

Twin headlights appear at the lip of the valley, momentarily piercing the fog with yellow, bouncing shafts, and as the vehicle turns, the shafts swing, drop, and disappear.

It's a pickup truck, and the driver moves a foot to the brake pedal, then the clutch as well, and drops it into second gear. The truck is creeping now, the wipers beating back and forth, squealing a little as they rub the mist away. The engine whines as it holds back, and the headlights poke holes of only two or three feet in the damp shroud.

The driver lowers the window and moves over to rest an arm on the door, as if to sense the distance of the truck from the edge of the road. The driver edges a little to the left. This is the hill side. The drop-off is to the right. The trees have arched over the road here, and the headlights show nothing. Sensing rather than seeing the switchback, the driver eases the wheel to the right, then all the way around. The dark shapes can be seen on both sides, and the driver edges to the right, for this is the safe side now. The right front wheel starts to drop, and the driver pulls to the left and then straightens up. The fog has thickened, and there are no dark shapes to act as guides. The truck rolls ahead blindly for another ten feet and comes to a stop.

Putting the engine in neutral and pulling on the handbrake, the driver gets out of the truck and walks hesitantly and searchingly to one edge of the road, then is suddenly silhouetted crossing in front of the truck to find the opposite edge. The driver comes back to the middle and walks down the center, away from the truck. A gray shape disappearing into the fog for perhaps ten or twelve paces, then slowly coming back into focus.

Straightening up again in the lights of the truck, the solitary figure stands still and listens. A faraway, muffled roar like that of a train or a truck on a highway comes up from below and seems to fade out. There is a rustling in the brush at the side of the road. The figure turns. A bird's wing fluttering through the leaves. A squirrel chatters tentatively in an unseen tree, and the figure raises its head to where the sound came from.

As if on signal, the fog begins to move slowly and silently. The trees emerge on the side of the road, and the faraway, muffled roar rises again from below. The squirrel chatters again, this time with greater assurance as the first pale shafts of light touch the treetops.

The figure turns towards the truck and bends down to look at a wristwatch in the glare of a headlight, as if not wanting to be late for an appointment, then gets back in, pulling the door shut quietly.

It's easier to see now, and the driver lets the truck roll more freely. Little wisps of cloud slip into the open window as the truck goes through the next switchback, takes the straightaway a little faster, and slows again as the driver brakes and dips into another. Each time the muffled roar grows louder, until it finally fills the air in an all-encompassing crescendo. Branches swipe at the truck's side as the driver pulls up and stops in what is now only a little more than an old logging trail. The driver gets out and stands with a hand still on the door.

The darkness and fog have lifted. Shafts of light seep into the ravine, and there are more muted sounds close by of birds and animals.

Then, as if breaking the spell, the driver closes the door without latching it and, reaching into the bed of the truck, lifts out a large, galvanized bucket. Bucket in hand, the driver walks down an obscure path to a small beach of brown sand, where the river turns and the current forms an eddy. Upriver, perhaps fifty yards, a torrent of water thunders between two huge rocks, slipping and sliding from one to the other and finally plunging into the pool like the run-off from a giant turbine. Spray fills the air as the current takes the sharp turn beneath the fall and heaves up mightily against an outcropping of rock from the side of the river. Bull Sluice.

The figure watches as if transfixed, and listens, but the air is now filled with one sound only. Setting the bucket on the sand, the figure studies the water, looks across the river at the dimly visible opposite bank perhaps one hundred feet away, then downriver where it swirls and bends out of sight.

Nothing else to hear, no more to see. The plan cannot fail. Jaynes will come through the sluice in ten minutes or less. He will come when beckoned over to this beach. He will run the canoe up on the sand, step out, and reach down to pull the canoe up. When he reaches down he will be without a helmet, and the back of his head will be fully exposed. That is when it will be done.

Slowly and deliberately now, the figure moves along

the edge of the brown sand. Finding a rock about the size of a grapefruit, the figure lifts it in one hand, weighing it, calculating, and then places it on the sand at the waterline. The process is repeated until there are four large stones spaced perhaps six feet apart along the perimeter of the brown beach. No time to look for a rock. One must be close by, handy. Straightening up, the figure looks at each one carefully and then back again at the sluice.

With a glance at the wristwatch, the figure returns to the bucket, turns it upside down, and sits down to wait.

3

Billy Birdsong

BILLY BIRDSONG WAS traveling along Highway 75 between Clayburn and Linville. The needle on the speedometer set rigidly on fifty-five as he made the sweeping turns, climbing up small grades and around the base of high mountains. The sun was burning through the early morning fog, doing its best to change from a misty silver dollar to a warm, golden sphere.

Billy was a Cherokee Indian, thin, medium height, maybe five-ten or eleven, but he still had had a basketball scholarship to the junior college. Billy never worried. Instead, he worked and smiled. Even when he brought someone in for an offense, he always referred to him as "my friend here," and meant it. He liked people, and generally when they got to know him, people liked him. That's why McPhee, the sheriff, had made him chief deputy, even over Lucas, who had more seniority. Even Lucas liked him now.

He lounged in the seat and looked at the asphalt two-laned road, the trees, rounded hills, and occasionally up to the higher peaks beyond. It was a Sunday, and he was on his way to work. He rolled the window down. Briggs hadn't been able to make it so he said he'd take his shift.

Nothing wrong with that, but Julie had complained. Only a little, though, and she had dutifully made him a fine stack with hot, spicy sausages, and kissed him so he knew it when he left.

He smiled to himself about the way she complained. Always on his side. "A chief deputy shouldn't have to work three out of four Sundays," Julie had said. But she said "chief deputy" like it was president of General Motors, and it always made him feel good. She knew he didn't like going to church much, but she never said it. Neither did he, but he went once in a while. Maybe they'd go to that new steak house tonight, and a show. There was supposed to be a good one on about some Alaskan wolves. Trouble was, there was so much junk he was almost afraid to take the boy. Well, he'd check when he got to the office.

Something up ahead in the middle of the road. Two vultures. Billy slowed down and the birds took off. He pulled over on the shoulder of the road. Raccoon, not too flat yet.

He glanced up and down the road, then got out, went over, picked it up by one hind leg, and carried it back to the front of the cruiser. Nice bushy tail. The boy would like that. He put the coon down, reached in his back pocket for his jacknife, and deftly severed the tail. Picking up the coon once more by the leg, he looked up and down the road. A car was approaching from behind him on his side. He moved the coon slightly behind him on the off side and curled the tail up in his hand. Then he put on his law and order face and watched the car go by as if inspecting its driver and contents for possible violations or contraband.

Once it was out of sight, Billy swung the dead coon around his head and let it fly into the bushes. Getting back in the cruiser, he put the tail in the glove compartment on top of his maps and snapped the cover shut. As he pulled out, he saw the vultures dip low and start to circle over the bushes.

He didn't have to pick up the coon, but call the S.P.C.A instead? Maybe they'd have come and maybe not. And meantime, "thrump, thrump," those cars would have been violating that little body. And the boy would like the tail.

The road was dropping away now, down to the bridge. Billy glanced in the rearview mirror and slowed down as he started across. Maybe some of the whitewater boys would be coming down. He'd come down a few times himself, but Julie didn't like it.

His eye caught a patch of red in the weeds on the far side. He slowed further and looked again. Something down there. He couldn't see it now. He pulled off in a little turn around at the end of the bridge. Looking at his watch, he saw that it was almost nine. So he'd be a little late.

He got out of the car, adjusted his belt, and circled around in front and went down the path. Probably an old T-shirt with some dumb saying. Billy shook his head and picked his way easily and surefootedly down to the river's edge. Nothing. No red T-shirt.

Here the river was wide and shallow. He looked across to the far shore, maybe a couple of hundred feet away. The rays of the morning sun were finding their way down now, and they glistened and sparkled on the water. He took off his hat and stood there like he was in a holy place. Billy had known this river since he was a boy. He'd swum in it, fished the hidden pools for rainbow trout, and hunted its woods for deer, coon and squirrel. It was a beautiful river. Years back the government had bought up all the lands on both sides to keep it that way.

He looked upstream. There were high peaks and hidden valleys up there. Coves, they called them here in the Smokies. The river started high up there and dropped four thousand feet in forty miles. Like a big, wet, curling snake it came rushing down through the valleys and ravines. No towns, no cottages, no roads, no people. Just a few hiking trails and places to put in or take out for people who liked to run the whitewater in rafts, canoes, or kayaks. It was very beautiful, and very dangerous.

Billy put his hat back on and fished an empty beer can out of the high grass. He followed the path up a small rise, and then he saw it. A patch of red down in the weeds. The beer can still in one hand, he pushed his way through the weeds and brush. He could see it now. One end of a red canoe sunk down in the water with just a foot or two showing. The rest was underwater.

He dropped the beer can and being careful to get only one foot a little wet, Billy guided the canoe out a little, then back in so he could get a grip on it. He grasped the canoe with one hand and dragged it to the shore. Then, bending over and grabbing the prow, he pulled it about halfway up. Two blocks of foam came loose that had evidently been tied in the front. Extra flotation.

Billy watched as the water drained out. There was a hole the size of a fist in the other end. He straightened up and looked around. A paddler in a canoe was coming under the bridge, and Billy waved him over.

The paddler picked his way across the current and between the rocks until the canoe touched bottom. He dug his paddle into the river bottom and held the canoe motionless. Billy checked him out: extra flotation, helmet, life jacket, shorts, a sweatshirt, a stubby beard, and steel-rimmed glasses.

"Stove-in canoe," said Billy, gesturing with his hand. "You see anything?"

"No, nothin'. Lots of rocks." The puddler looked back over his shoulder up the river.

"Mm." Billy looked down at the canoe. "Thought maybe somebody had trouble."

"Maybe just drifted out by itself." He was lean, stringy-looking, no kid, maybe thirty-five.

"Where'd you put in?" Billy smiled at him.

"Bateman's Ford. Been on the river about an hour, maybe more."

"Anybody in the parking lot when you left?"

"Nobody." He gave a slight shake of his head.

"Pretty early for most people, I guess," said Billy.

"It's better when you got the river to yourself. See more game, too. Saw couple deer up back."

Billy nodded, "Yeah." He looked down again at his stove-in canoe.

"You local?"

"No, Atlanta."

"You got your ticket?" Billy referred to the departure ticket that everybody filled out, then left a copy in the box where they put in. The man changed hands on the paddle, reached in his back pocket, took out a wallet, picked out the ticket, and held it out. Billy leaned over and took it. Taking out his notebook, he copied down the name, address, point of departure, and destination. "Says here, two in the party."

"Partner is a little ahead of me." He motioned down the river.

Billy started to pass it back, and stopped. "You know, according to regulations, I'm supposed to check this ticket with some identification. You got a driver's license?" He still held the ticket in his hand and proffered it, but only halfway, suggesting he'd give up the ticket when he got the license.

The paddler picked at the wallet again and passed a license up to Billy. The license checked with the name on the ticket. Billy passed them back.

"Well, have a nice trip." He waved him on.

"Thanks. I'll keep an eye out."

"Yeah." Billy watched him move out to deep water,

into the current, and around the bend. He started up the bank, then stopped, and went back to the river's edge and picked up the beer can. He could hear the sluice now, faintly in the distance. It was just upstream aways and around a bend. All thc danger spots on the river were labeled on the government charts from I to VI. Only two places were bad enough to be called Whitewater VI. One was the Eye of the Needle, and the other was Bull Sluice.

Billy knew the numbers. Twenty-two killed on the river, and half at the sluice. He dropped the beer can in the canoe and started upriver.

Slowly he made his way along the bank until he came to a little slough that branched off from the main current. He was moving along the path perhaps five minutes up from the bridge, and the sound of the sluice was getting louder. Stopping, he pushed the brush to one side for a better look, and there it was. A man's body floating facedown. Those yellow life jackets weren't supposed to let a man float facedown, but there he was, legs and arms spread-eagled like a sky diver before he pulled the rip cord.

Billy jerked into life. He scrambled down, waded out, and grabbed the man beneath the armpits. He dragged him up on the bank and started to roll him over. Then he saw the wound at the back of the head. A rock wound. He reached out and touched the little place where there was matted hair and blood, and then he gently laid the head on its side, so its weight would not rest on the wound.

Taking his revolver from the holster, he shot into the sky three times quickly, then three more. He slid the gun back in his holster and went to work trying to revive the man. He felt sure he knew him from somewhere.

4

The Sheriff

PETER McPHEE SAT on the edge of the back porch and reached down for a dirty pair of sneakers labeled "Adidas." The dog sat in the grass, watching him closely: small dog, liver and white, big ears, plenty of feathering, a Brittany, eyes glued to every move McPhee made. One sneaker on. Laces tied up. Then the other, a little trouble with the heel. Finger in the back, there that's it. Two on. Two laced up. This could be it. The dog moved impulsively six inches towards the field, holding himself in check, and raised his eyes to McPhee's. He was full of it and ready, like a racehorse in the starting gate. McPhee got to his feet, hitched up the shorts, gave the sweatshirt one last pull, and stepped onto the dew-wet grass.

"Okay." He said it almost under his breath, like a man who had just got out of bed and who wasn't sure what the new day might hold for him. The dog exploded with pent-up energy and bounded to one side, then the other, high in the air, then came down with both legs flat out in front, head laid on top of the legs. And when he saw McPhee break into an easy jog, he tore out and away towards the end of the pasture, like a bullet, to where the grass was tall. He took to leaping then, with front legs laid back like a small deer so that he could see over and beyond the grass. And then he came back in a wide circle, belly low to ground, reaching hard and fast with all four legs, ears caught in the wind, almost straight out. He circled McPhee and took off again, this time a little slower, stopping by the corner of the barn to leave his mark. After a furious dig and scuff session, when he scraped one foot at a time, making grass and dirt fly behind him, he took off again for the creek.

McPhee was moving easily now, and the early morning chill was slowly giving way to a little inside warmth. The peaks of the mountains beyond the creek were barely visible through the fog and mist, and small patches still hung low over the trees and bushes bordering the creek. He headed down toward an opening in the brush where the creek widened and shallowed out with brown sand and small rock piles, breaking the one little stream into three or four smaller ones. Slowing down, he picked his way across as the dog splashed through beside him. Then it was up the bank on a path along the stream where he could see through the branches of the sycamores and poplars, to his house and barn and shed sitting on a knoll in the distance. It gave him a warm feeling to look at it, and think about it. It was his place.

The dog came sliding down the mountain side of the path, stopped in the middle of it to check on McPhee, who was now pumping along in a light sweat. Satisfied, the dog took off into the brush again. A moment later McPhee heard the heavy whirr of wings, and the dog yelped twice. Grouse. They were always up on this side of the hill. He started humming to himself for a little company and a little rhythm, picking up his feet and putting them down in time with his own music. It helped move him along.

He came to the place where the path turned back to the creek. The banks were high here, but an old pine had fallen, bridging the creek. He picked his way across

He'd come back from Nam and found that most of his friends had left for "bigger towns and bigger bucks." That was the thing to do, so you did it. His folks wanted him to finish college, so he went down to Atlanta and enrolled at Emory. He'd thought of going into law, but he'd read about some chief justice who made a speech saying that the country was crawling with lawyers, so he took a degree in Business Administration.

Sold insurance for a while. He went to meetings, seminars, and worked hard. He had an easy way with people, did what he was told, said what they wanted him to say, and he made good money. Got himself a nicer apartment and a sports car. Had a few girls, some serious, some not too serious, but fun. He'd started eating at the better restaurants, and even got to know the names of some of the wines he liked. He was living the good life.

Then his daddy died and he came home. His mother told him that the farm was his along with three thousand dollars, which was his share of the insurance after they took out for the farm. He said that was just fine.

She said she was going to California to live with his sister, who had three kids, a job as a dental hygienist, and a part-time husband. He said he understood, and that was fine too.

He drove her to the airport in Ashville, kissed her good-bye, and watched her get on the plane, Piedmont, Flight 401, and he got tears in his eyes. He'd said he'd fly out for Christmas, but he never did. Three years ago, it was.

He rolled down the window of the car, made the turn onto the highway, and settled back a little. The sun was burning through the fog, and he could see the tops of the faraway ranges. McPhee liked the drive in to town. He thought it was beautiful. Sunday looked like it was going to be a nice day.

He pulled into the slot marked Sheriff and went into the back door of the county building. His department shared it with the tax assessor, the tax collector, the county agricultural agent, social services, and you name it. It was not a large building. Thc halls were empty. Real quiet. Almost too quiet.

Simmons was at the dispatcher's desk. It was just a little cubicle off the front office. The court calendar hung to one side with the court dates marked in yellow. A big map of the county hung next to it, just above the counter. Three sets of padlocked files, three chairs, and a standing wooden ashtray faced a four-foot counter, all a little tacky and tired. On the bulletin board behind the counter were various notices and a whole pad of F.B.I. "wanted" posters, bound together like a book. In the center of the bulletin board was a bronze plaque. It read:

This is not Burger King.
We do not do it your way.
We do it our way.
And so will you.

The former sheriff had put it there and McPhee left it, for the time being. He'd only had the job three months. McPhee didn't like it, though. It ought to come down.

"You all alone?"

"Billy called in and said he'd take over for Briggs today." He looked at the clock that read quarter after nine and then back at the pad he was writing on.

Simmons was a good man, but he was not big on eye contact. "He should be in any minute."

"Anybody out back?" He was referring to the six cells just behind the office space.

"Trooper brought in a D.U.I. about four this morning. He's sleeping it off." The State Patrol used his jail when they had to, and so did the city police department.

without looking at the rocks and pools some ten or fifteen feet below. At the far end he looked over his shoulder to reassure himself, and saw the dog take the log at a full trot.

When he got back to the house, the red light was on at the bottom of the coffee pot. He wiped his face with a towel, poured some hot and black, and stood a minute, sipping. The house was quiet. He let his eyes run over the fireplace, the books, and the stereo. She thought the fireplace was dirty, the books a waste of time, and the only music they agreed on was Willie Nelson and Anne Murray. She wasn't even sure about Anne Murray. And the TV? He'd even bought a satellite dish, but that didn't do it, either.

The bedroom door was open. He could see the double bed. One side unmade. The other obviously not slept in. Three weeks since she had left. He reached over, filled his cup again, and pulled the plug on the pot. He looked out through the screen door where the dog sat watching him.

"We don't know what she wanted, do we, Brook? I don't think she did, either!"

The dog cocked his head to one side at the mention of his name. She was over in Raleigh now, taking a few graduate courses and working part-time as a legal secretary. She'd get along. She'd get along all right, with that long, red hair and those hips that moved like Mother Earth. She carried herself like an Indian princess in prime time. Easy eyes and confident, mostly. He looked through the open door to the bedroom again and stretched. He thought back to other Sunday mornings when he didn't have to go in, especially before he'd been elected, and a little grin spread across his face. He sipped some more coffee, roused himself, and ran his hand through his hair. He scratched what he thought might be a chigger bite under his right arm.

Going over to the sink he emptied his cup, rinsed it out, and hung it on the hook with three others. Under the sink he scooped out some Purina Chow and went out on the porch and poured it in the dog dish. The dog was nowhere around. McPhee looked off down the pasture and saw him standing motionless, on a point. He took off his sneakers slowly when the dog continued to hold, waiting a moment to see what the dog had. Nothing. Then he turned and padded barefoot back into the house to shave, shower, and go into town. The screen door banged behind him.

The road wound down the little valley, or cove, through dense sections of hardwood: poplar, maple, walnut, some oak, and pine up on the hills. Small farms here and there, knee-high corn, some tobacco, and plenty of small patches of tomatoes and beans, a few white-faced cattle, some black and white milk cows, and an occasional apple or peach orchard starting to bloom. White houses with porches and rusty tin roofs, usually on a rise or tucked back into a mountain with a view in front and a spring in back. Not much as farming country went, but you could get by with a little county mowing and repairing for the summer folks up from Florida. That's the way his daddy had made it.

Things were changing now. The younger ones took jobs in the growing number of small plants. Most of them made jeans, shirts, blouses; a few of the newer and larger ones were in electronics. Good steady labor, no unions, tax breaks, all kinds of help from the county, and good security.

McPhee took the turns a little left, around to the right, then back left again and up over a rise, eyes on the double white line, Always double. There wasn't a mile of straight and level road in the county, and still some of the younger ones in their pickups and roll bars with the two spotlights on top drove these roads like the Daytona 500.

McPhee looked at the duty roster. If Billy was taking over, he sould have been here twenty minutes ago. Not like Billy.

"Give him a call if he doesn't show up in a little while. I'm going for breakfast."

He went out the front door of the county building and paused on the front steps. The sun was bright after the dark of the hallway. The old courthouse was opposite, in the middle of the square. The square was deserted. A few cars over by the Baptist church, but it was still a little early for church people.

McPhee was almost six feet tall, but that's where it ended. He was not broad shouldered, and he did not walk like John Wayne. He did not wear a uniform—he dressed casually in slacks, sport shirt, and a jacket. He did not even have the boyish sincerity of Jimmy Stewart. Had he worn glasses, he could have been mistaken for a studious professor at a small liberal arts college who was reluctant to flunk anyone. The fellow who ran against him for sheriff had made that mistake. He'd said if McPhee was "lean and mean" instead of "lean and green" he might make a good sheriff. That did it! McPhee beat him by six lengths going away. Won an election and lost a wife. Who knew what was smart these day? Maybe he should have stayed with insurance.

He went down the steps and across the street to the hotel. It was an old hotel with a new coffee shop. It had a carved wooden sign with old English lettering like a tavern: Keebler House, Travelers Rest. Trains stopped there in the old days for thirty minutes so passengers could have lunch. Food was still good. Listed in the Travelers Guide, with four stars.

Courtney Carpenter and Spurgeon Foss were sitting towards the back. The town square was dominated by four large, well-kept buildings: the courthouse, the Baptist church, the county building, and the Foss Funeral

Home. Foss was heavyset, solid, in his mid-forties, with a full head of prematurely gray hair.

Courtney was something else. He alternated three suits—dark brown, dark blue and dark gray, all well tailored. After he wore one, he hung it in the other end of the closet to keep track. He was retired and a widower who took all his meals at the Keebler House. He ate there not only because the food was good but also because he owned the place.

It was cool inside. Had style. Linen tablecloths and real chrysanthemums on each table. Courtney pulled out a chair for McPhee. He liked the young sheriff.

Courtney had a linen napkin tucked into his vest and had gone back to carefully maneuvering a little peach cobbler onto his spoon to go with a little vanilla ice cream that was already there. He looked up at McPhee. "Anybody rob the bank last night?"

"Nobody mentioned it if they did."

McPhee sat down and ordered two eggs over easy, toast, and coffee.

Foss said, "Probably nobody'd know about it."

McPhee grinned. "How come you keep company like this, Courtney?"

The old man dabbed at his mustache with the napkin. "Can't be too choosy this early on a Sunday morning. Just not that many people around." He enjoyed his own little joke and took a sip of coffee.

The waitress brought McPhee's eggs, and he buttered a little toast to go with them. She poured more coffee for Courtney, and he thanked her. She then moved around to Foss, but he put his hand over his cup and looked at McPhee.

"Anything at all going on in the sheriff's department?"

McPhee shook his head. "Nothing. Real quiet. Just one of those D.U.I.'s last night. Sleeping it off."

He said it without thinking, and Spurgeon Foss adjusted himself a little in his chair. It was only two weeks ago that young Spur had been picked up with a half-empty bottle in the front seat. Somehow he'd mistaken a runaway truck ramp for the right-hand lane as he was coming down the mountain, and came to a stop up to his hubcaps in sand. He was asleep when they found him, so the prosecutor dropped the charges. But it was a sensitive thing. The three of them sat quietly for a moment. It was almost like a silent tribute to Foss and his problem. The judge, sensing his uneasiness, wiped his mustache.

"Ought to try that cobbler, Spurgeon. Real good."

Spurgeon shook his head. "I just can't eat breakfast. A little coffee and toast suits me, but my stomach can't take it." He looked around for understanding, and Courtney and McPhee both nodded.

Simmons was coming in the front door. He looked hurriedly around, spotted them, and made for their table. A little fast for Simmons.

"Billy called in. He wants to talk to you."

"Right now?"

Simmons caught the sheriff's eyes and held them for a moment. "Yeah. He's holdin'." Then he glanced at the judge and Foss.

"I'll be right with you." McPhee took the last piece of toast, swallowed the rest of his coffee, and stood up.

"Enjoyed it."

Courtney looked at him and smiled.

Simmons waited while McPhee left the money at the unattended register.

"Billy's got a body down in the river by the highway. He thinks it's some big executive at the electronics plant."

That could mean a lot of things, and none of them were good. McPhee was at home with local people. Electronics executives, he didn't know too many.

"He thinks he drowned but he's not sure."

That got McPhee's full attention even though he didn't know what it meant. The muscles at the back of his neck tightened a little, and he gave his belt a hitch.

"Oh?" He kept his pace deliberately slow and even as he walked across thc street to the county building with Simmons at his elbow.

5

Jay Jay Jaynes

THERE WERE PERHAPS twenty people standing by the end of the bridge, and the medics were backing the ambulance slowly towards the crowd when McPhee arrived. Some cars had pulled off on each side of the road, while the rest of the traffic had slowed down to see what it was all about. Pulling up just beyond the ambulance, McPhee spotted the ranger coming across the road and asked him to keep the traffic moving.

Billy was down the bank by the edge of the river, and the medics were bent over a figure laid out on the ground. One of the ambulance men was attaching an inhalator, while the other was making ready to give a shot.

McPhee moved up next to Billy. "How's he doing?"

Billy shook his head. "I think he's long gone, but you never know."

McPhee edged around to look at the victim's face. "Do you know who he is? Any I.D.?"

Billy shrugged his shoulders. "Looks like that guy that runs the electronics plant, Jones, Jaynes, something like that."

It was an electronics plant, Contel, that had located in the valley about four years before. Came in, bought sixty acres one half-mile off the highway, built a beautiful, modern complex complete with chain link fence and twenty-four-hour guards, and employed about four hundred people. McPhee had heard that it was owned by a West German firm, and they operated another five or six plants in the southeast. He ran it all through his mind.

Since that time they had built a research plant and administrative offices for American affairs. And then, to top it all off, they bought another thirty thousand acres as a real estate development: Emerald Valley, complete with golf course, ski lift, lake, trout hatchery, stables, tennis courts, clubhouse, and helicopter pad. Said they wanted an executive community for their people, but it was open to qualified buyers who just wanted to live there. Developed lot prices started at fifty thousand dollars, which effectively qualified most buyers, with maintenance and all privileges amounting to about one thousand dollars per month. And Jay Jay Jaynes had been the mover and shaker.

The man's face was covered with the mask of the inhalator, and the medics were preparing to put him on the stretcher. McPhee walked over closer. The face was bruised, and with the man holding the inhalator in place, it was hard to see. There were abrasions around the knees. The knee pads had slipped down and lay loose around his ankles. The body had a puffy look to it already, and the skin was white.

Billy had moved over with him.

"Have a life jacket, helmet?"

"I took the jacket off, but I didn't see a helmet."

Billy patted the back of his head. "Cut back there on his head. They say he liked to run the river."

"Hm." He looked at the body again. Black, curly hair and prominent nose, maybe forty, slim, good shoulders. It looked like Jaynes.

Billy was at his side as he stepped back. "You recognize him too?"

"Yeah. I think so."

McPhee bent over and spoke to the medics. One gave a slight shake of his head. The sheriff straightened up a little as he saw a young, bearded man with a TV camera and a sling bag over his shoulder approaching. He was with a young girl in jeans and an open-necked shirt.

"What is it, Sheriff?" The girl stopped in front of him and smiled.

She had a mike in her hand. The bearded man had the camera on his shoulder now. He was pointing it at McPhee, alternately looking through it and then adjusting the lens. It hadn't taken them long. You had to give them that. McPhee took a deep breath and let it out slowly.

The young girl held the mike in front of him, and he felt a knot fully formed now in the pit of his stomach. He motioned Billy over with one hand and locked his thumb over his belt buckle near the knot.

"We need a statement, Sheriff." She moved the mike closer.

McPhee looked straight into the camera. "At nine this morning, Chief Deputy Birdsong saw something in the river as he crossed the bridge. When he investigated he found a canoe with a hole in it. He looked further up the river and found a man with his head down in the water. He pulled him out, gave mouth-to-mouth resuscitation, and called for the ambulance. That's all we know at present."

"Has he been identified, Sheriff?"

"No, ma'am."

"Was he wearing a life jacket and helmet?"

The sheriff looked at Billy, and the bearded one moved the camera onto the chief deputy.

Billy said, "He was wearing a life jacket but no helmet when I found him."

"Any response from the victim?"

McPhee took over. "We're doing everything we can, and when we have additional information, we'll give it to you."

"Were there any signs of life?"

McPhee looked down at the ground. He didn't like the question. He looked back up at the camera. "We're doing all we can, and so are the medics. When we learn more of the facts, we'll certainly give them to you. Thank you."

Why did they have to be so damn pushy?

"That was Sheriff Peter McPhee and Chief Deputy Birdsong reporting on an accident that occurred this morning at the Highway 75 bridge over the Chatooga River, and this is Delia Hartman with your local TV Station WIRS, where news comes first."

The bearded one relaxed, and Billy and McPhee watched the ambulance pull away. The small gathering drifted apart.

Billy looked at him. "Why me?"

McPhee gave half a shrug. "You found the body."

They walked slowly down to the canoe. The life jacket was lying nearby. McPhee had gotten a little reaction when he appointed Billy chief deputy. Two or three folks had asked if he knew Billy was a full-blooded Cherokee. McPhee said, "Yes, I knew it," and let it go at that.

Billy picked up the jacket, shaking his head. "It's supposed to keep the head out of water if the victim is unconscious. Maybe in a pool or a calm ocean, but whitewater?" He dropped it in the canoe.

McPhee nodded.

"You were right about that being the fellow from the electronics plant. His name is Jaynes. I met him before, and I think he liked to run the river. You look around for the helmet."

They both started slowly up the path above the river. As they rounded the curve past where the body was found, the roar of the sluice hit their ears. A little, brown sandy beach was opposite, and they stood surveying the scene, looking for the helmet or whatever.

Billy said, "I'm going to take a look. I'll be back in a minute." He took off to his car as McPhee watched. He saw Billy turn and drive the cruiser across the bridge.

McPhee went back up the road. The crowd had pretty well dispersed, and the ranger was talking to a man and his wife.

"I was just telling these folks that this is the fourth fatality we've had at the sluice in the past three years. It can be dangerous."

McPhee nodded. "I wonder, could your people get that canoe and the jacket up to the Information Building for me?"

"Sure thing. We'll keep it up there till you come and get it. By the way, Sheriff, that fellow probably wrote a put in ticket somewhere up the line."

"That's right. You suppose you could get it for me?"

"No trouble, Sheriff. Glad to help."

McPhee thought for a minute. "You might bring them all down."

"Sure, I'll get 'em."

McPhee walked over to his car and picked up the mike. "Simmons, this is the sheriff. The victim was sent to the county hospital at 9:50 A.M. No positive I.D., and the medics were still working on him . . . No, I don't think so. Billy's still with me . . . No, I'll be out until maybe noon. Give Mrs. Owens a ring. I'm sure she'll come over to cover. Okay?"

Billy pulled up next to him as he replaced the mike. "I found this, Sheriff. It was floating in the weeds." He held out a small oilskin pouch about the size of a wallet.

McPhee opened it, and inside were two twenty-dollar

bills and a "put in" ticket. The ticket was wet but legible. "Put in" time was 7:20 A.M.; location of entry, Bateman's Ford; location of exit, Millard's Shoals; number in party, blank; and there was the name half-printed, half-written, J. J. Jaynes, the mover and shaker who had stopped doing both about thirty minutes earlier.

6

Gloria and Company

THE DECK ON the house was tremendous; perhaps twenty-four feet wide by sixty feet long. It projected out over the valley for its full twenty-four feet, being supported by four steel I beams cantilevered out from the solid rock formation upon which the house sat. The beams had been bolted and welded to steel embedded in the rock. Since the drop-off was close to fifteen hundred feet almost straight down, the effect was strikingly dramatic.

While admiring a sunset, or the cloud formations against the distant peaks, one or two of a number of guests gathered at the rail could always be seen slipping back unobtrusively towards the house. They just were not sure the deck could support all that weight with nothing visible underneath to hold it up. Jay Jay would spot the unbelievers and launch into his story of how the firm of architects that designed the house was the best in the country, how the steel had been trucked up the mountain, the holes bored in the solid rock, and last of all, how the deck in its entirety had been insured by Lloyd's of London in the amount of five hundred thousand dollars for its structural integrity over a period of twenty-five years. "This, of course," he would always add, "was in addition to the regular policy of one million on the house."

Inevitably this was followed by an impressive silence, after which someone would jump up and down a little and say, "It certainly feels safe, Jay Jay, doesn't jiggle at all." And a few would laugh politely a little and wander off to enjoy the feeling of being suspended among the clouds and peaks. Others would move back surreptitiously to freshen up their drinks or pick at the hors d'oeuvres.

Four large sets of glass sliding doors led onto the deck. Three of these were rolled out of sight, pocketed at each side, while the fourth led to the master bedroom. It was a stunning, breathtaking arrangement, and visitors from all over the world compared it most favorably with anything they had ever seen.

On this Sunday morning the deck was almost empty. At one end, four people were grouped around a large, circular glass coffee table. The top was supported by a uniquely shaped and smoothly finished tree limb with branches.

Gloria Jaynes had taken off the pants and jacket of her jogging suit and was lounging next to the table in blue and white shorts with a matching tank top. Although she was in her mid-thirties, her body could have passed for that of a late, but full-blooming teenager. The shorts were slit up the sides, fully revealing two well-tanned, long, tawny limbs in their entirety. The tank top let it be known that she was wearing nothing underneath. Her hair was in two long, blonde braids, and her eyes had a habitual amused look, as if she was continually watching her ship come in. Even now, as she gazed at the mountains.

Off to one side, beneath a large deck umbrella, Morgan Lochmiller, executive vice president of Lumeniere, the corporate parent of Contel, was spread out in a deck chair. He was a huge man; his massive body blotted out the chair completely. Long salt-and-pepper hair was brushed straight back from all around his face—he could have passed for an aging Metro-Goldwyn-Mayer lion. It also gave him a somewhat scholarly look. His eyes were deep set and crinkled from smiling, smiling that kept the world at bay and betrayed nothing at all of his real thoughts, ever. Even now, as he idly observed Gloria's tank top, one could not be absolutely sure of what was in his mind. He still seemed preoccupied, and occasionally he looked appraisingly at the others.

Joe Bradham, the local manager, was over fifty, and up-front all the way. He wore white, well-tailored slacks and a pale yellow sport shirt. Bradham played golf three or four times a week, and always put his chip shots within three feet of the cup. He also talked well, concise, humorous, and almost always amiably agreeable. He moved with an agile grace despite a little midriff bulge, and with his bald head and clipped mustache, he was the quintessence of casual efficiency. He had just offered the front-page section of the *Atlanta Constitution* to Lochmiller, but Locky had declined with a shake of his head.

Ruth Bradham, his wife, was still a beautiful woman. She, too, was over fifty. This morning she was smartly groomed in sleekly tailored cream slacks, light blue sweater, and a yellow scarf. She wore dark glasses, however, for she was still slightly hung over from the party of the night before.

Locky liked to get his "family" together once every two months, and he frequently chose this place to do it. He said it was like the Bavarian Alps, only friendlier, and with not so many people. The other party guests had flown out the night before; now the reunion was over.

Gloria got up from the lounge chair and poured Locky

some coffee, leaving him in no doubt as to what was beneath the tank top. She still held the pot. "Ruth? Joe?"

Mrs. Bradham shook her head, but Joe came over with his cup. While she was pouring he selected a Danish roll from an assortment on the table. A golden retriever that had been lying in the middle of the deck roused himself to look at the bun in Bradham's hand. Gloria put the coffee pot back and gave Locky her full attention.

"I can't believe that you actually got up at that early hour, rode over with Jay Jay in the pickup, and then found your way back. No trouble at all, Locky?"

"Well, I suppose it depends on what you mean by 'trouble,' my dear." He emptied the contents of a little packet of sweetener in the coffee, and stirred the coffee slowly while looking at it.

"Coming back was easy. I turned right, crossed the little bridge over the river, and followed the dirt road to a paved road and got lost. So then I got out the map. When all else fails, read the directions. Then I came home."

Bradham broke off a piece of his bun, and the dog got up and went over to get it. "The roads are terrible, but the maps are good."

"Exactly. No trouble at all. I came right to our valley. But going over was the trouble. Jay Jay was driving and fog was on the road. Up and down we go and around this way and that way, and you could hardly see the front fenders sometimes. I said to him, 'Jay Jay, I take it you have never met anybody on this road?' 'Why's that?' he says.

"Because if you did, you'd both be dead and you wouldn't be here now."

He laughed at his little joke, and the others smiled. Bradham stood watching him closely and appreciatively. When Locky stopped laughing and looked up at

Bradham, Bradham asked, "You're sure he doesn't have a radar set into the dashboard? You know Jay Jay is always one jump ahead."

"I think I know Jay Jay, but maybe he does have a radar in his head. Anyway, he got off all right. I helped him with the canoe and off he went."

Ruth Bradham lit a cigarette and looked at Lochmiller. One leg was crossed over the other, and she began moving her foot up and down a little. "Everybody thinks they know Jay Jay, and then he's off and running again in a different direction."

Gloria looked at her with a touch of sympathy. Then she changed the subject. "See there," she pointed at the distant ridge, "you can see Black Mountain now, and it's going to be a beautiful day."

No one else picked it up.

Bradham went back to his chair and folded the newspapers. "Jay Jay is a mover and a shaker all right. He knows how to get things done."

Locky nodded slightly. "Exactly. A mover and shaker. Look what we have here. Five years ago a wilderness, and now way over fifty million and it's solid on the books. Jay Jay saw you didn't have to do business in the city. It's the age of communication. From here I call up my computer in West Germany. It says, 'Good morning, Mr. Lochmiller,' or 'Good afternoon,' depending on the time, right? And it tells me whatever I want to know." He looked at Bradham. "You got one too, right?"

"Right. Anything I want to know."

"We saw it and Jay Jay did it."

Bradham sensed a little inconsistency here. He couldn't recall Lochmiller's initiative at all, but he said, "Exactly." He knew it was a reassuring term.

Locky changed the subject. "How was the golf?"

"Great. Good game. On the third hole I chipped it right into the cup from a good forty feet. Birdie."

Gloria went back to Locky. "Did Jay Jay also con you into picking him up after his run this morning? After all, you have your maps and it's only about twelve miles down the river."

Locky looked at his watch. "I told him I'd be delighted to pick him up at eleven-thirty. Plenty of time. Besides, we have things to settle, things to talk about. I told him I'd be there, and I will."

The dog heard it first. He turned from Bradham, from whom he'd been patiently awaiting a second handout, and walked to the end of the deck. As the sound of the approaching car grew louder, Gloria got out of her chair and turned to go in through the living room. "More company."

The dog had growled and then began a steady, loud, full-bodied barking. Gloria stopped when she was almost through the door. "It's all right. Quiet. We know, now." The dog went back to growling and poked his head through the rails to see better.

McPhee would have liked to talked to Gloria Jaynes down in the entryway, but she insisted that both he and Billy come up on the deck. It was never easy, but this was going to be really difficult. He nodded politely as he was introduced. No one got out of their chairs, but they nodded back. He introduced Billy and sat in the proffered chair. The dog came over and gave McPhee a thorough and suspicious going-over and then went over and sat next to Billy, in the chair next to the sheriff.

No, he wouldn't have any coffee, and Billy also declined. McPhee didn't like all the company, but he didn't know what else to do but to follow her lead. Maybe it would be a little better this way, after all. At least she wasn't alone.

"Well, Mr. McPhee, as sheriff I take it this is an official visit. Did you want to see my husband, or what?"

McPhee took a notebook from his pocket, just to have something in his hands. "It's about your husband, Mrs. Jaynes. He did go down the river this morning, right?"

There was a silence that lasted for a full ten seconds as the tension peaked. Gloria Jaynes looked at her hands. "Yes, he did."

"There's been an accident. Your husband got a blow on the head from a river rock and drowned."

Mrs. Bradham grabbed the arms of her chair and stared at the sheriff in shock. Joe Bradham looked from McPhee to Gloria and back again. Gloria just went on looking at her hands. Lochmiller rolled his head to one side, his eyes narrowing as if taking stock of what had been said. He was the first to speak. "You are certain?"

The sheriff looked at Billy, who produced the still-wet pouch with the twenty dollar bills and signed "put in" ticket. He got up and brought them over to Mrs. Jaynes. She dropped her eyes from the sheriff, and took the pouch in her hands, and read the ticket. "These are Jay Jay's." She set them on the coffee table.

Billy had returned to his seat. "We found that nearby in the river."

Gloria Jaynes looked back at the sheriff. There was a question in her eyes.

McPhee returned her look and then lowered his eyes to the coffee table. "They did everything they could, but the hospital called us on our way over here. He was gone before they got him there."

Lochmiller asked, "How did it happen?"

"We don't really know. It was at Bull Sluice. It's one of the more dangerous spots on the river. Just below it

Billy found the body and the canoe with a hole in it. What time was it, Billy?"

"At about nine A.M. I spotted the canoe as I came over the bridge. Then I walked up the river just to look around, thinking somebody may have had some trouble, and I saw the orange life jacket."

Billy paused and looked around. They all were still looking at him. He glanced at McPhee, and it was evident that he, too, expected Billy to finish the story.

"Well, I pulled him out and laid him on the ground and shot my gun for help. I breathed into his mouth and all, and when another fella came I sent him for help. I worked on him until the ambulance came. He had a real bad cut in the back there." Billy held his hand up to the back of his own head to let them know where it was.

"The medics put the respirator on him and gave him a shot. After the ambulance took him away, I found the packet in the water." He pointed at the still-wet pouch lying on the coffee table.

Gloria Jaynes leaned over and picked up the pouch again and removed the permit. "I'm sure you people did all you could."

Billy said, "Thank you, ma'am."

She looked at the bottom of the permit and nodded her head. "That's his signature."

Lochmiller came over and Gloria handed the permit to him.

"Location of entry, Bateman's Ford; location of exit, Millard's Shoals; time of launch, seven twenty."

"Yes." His nod affirmed it to the group. "I watched him fill this out and put the white copy in the box. I asked him about the other side, number eight. It says that a minimum party size of two persons and two craft is required below Bateman's Ford."

He looked at the group, realizing that perhaps it was in

poor taste to bring up the idea of Jay Jay's apparent disregard of the regulations.

Gloria raised her eyes to Billy. "Was he wearing a helmet?"

"No, ma'am. I looked but couldn't find a helmet."

"Jay Jay liked going it alone, and he didn't like wearing a helmet. He said they were hot, heavy, and he couldn't hear as well. But he did usually wear one."

Lochmiller set the permit back on the coffee table. "Come to think of it, Jay Jay did search in the back of the pickup for that helmet. So did I."

They all looked at him.

He shrugged. "But we never found it. He didn't have it when he left."

Bradham spoke up. "There's been a number of fatalities on that river, haven't there, Sheriff?"

"Yes. I'm sorry to have to bring you this information, Mrs. Jaynes."

Gloria didn't look at him. She was looking at the permit. "Thank you, Sheriff, I understand."

Mrs. Bradham came over and sat beside her on the couch. "You going to be all right?"

"I think so."

Lochmiller spoke up again. "I thought he knew how to do this sort of thing. He must have gone down that river many times."

Bradham nodded. "Every Sunday if the weather wasn't too bad. But the river can be dangerous."

The sheriff cleared his throat. "The water was high, ma'am."

"That makes a difference?" asked Lochmiller.

"Yes. The river is faster, more water pouring through adds a lot to the danger."

Lochmiller looked at the sheriff. "There will be an official report on this accident?"

"Of course. Someone should make an identification as well. He's at Mercy Hospital."

"I'll go after a bit," Gloria Jaynes said.

Lochmiller started to object.

McPhee spoke up. "We like to have a close relative, if possible. You know where the hospital is located, Mrs. Jaynes?"

She nodded.

"Is there anything else we can tell you, or do for you?"

"No, Sheriff, I don't think so."

"Well, we're very sorry about this whole thing. Please call us if anything at all comes up where you think we can help." McPhee got up and Billy followed suit.

Bradham got up. "I'll show you out, Sheriff." As they walked through the living room to the entry hall, he added, "Jay Jay was good in a canoe, but I guess accidents can happen to anybody."

McPhee said, "That's right."

The door closed behind them, and they walked silently to the car. It was Billy's car, and he got into the driver's seat. McPhee slammed the door, and Billy reached over to put his notebook in the glove compartment.

The raccoon tail fell into McPhee's lap. Billy looked at him. "Bushy, eh?"

7

Bull Sluice

THEY WERE DRIVING back to the river parking lot where they had left McPhee's car.

"You know, Pete," Billy said—he called McPhee "Pete" only when they were alone. "Those people back there were different."

"They've got a lot of money, Billy."

"Yeah, but I know other people with a lot of money that aren't like that."

McPhee was wondering if he should order an autopsy, and he also wondered if he should ask Mrs. Jaynes or just go ahead with it. He was only half listening.

"What do you mean?"

"Not a sniffle. Not a tear. 'How did it happen? Was he wearing a helmet? Didn't he know there was a rule saying two to a party?' Is that the way *your* wife would act if you got killed?" The minute he said it he was sorry, but he could think of nothing to cover it right away.

"Honestly, Billy, I don't know."

"Well, what I mean is, normal circumstances, you know, man and wife."

"People are different. Some people don't react the same way you and I do." He was still thinking about the autopsy. What could it show anyway? He drowned.

"Yeah, but they were cold, McPhee, cold."

"Well, they learn to control their emotions. Your old dog dies, you get a new dog. You know."

Billy thought about this. It was true, but he remembered when their last dog got killed by a car. "Even our dog, though. Julie cried like a baby."

"But you got a new dog."

He looked at McPhee with the beginning of outrage. "She wouldn't stop crying. I had to."

McPhee looked out the window. He knew there were times when everybody felt a hurt, but covered up. It didn't necessarily mean they didn't feel it, especially if they'd been hurt many times. But he was still thinking about the autopsy. Maybe he should call Mrs. Jaynes first.

"People are different."

"I don't think they gave a damn. That's what I think."

McPhee thought about that. Mrs. Bradham was really the only one who seemed sorry. It did seem like they were pretty callous and were about to ask him what he'd done with the canoe. But it was an accident. Why bother with an autopsy? He looked out the window again. It was the same Sunday. Quiet. The sun warmed the day, the fields and woods were greening up, but when he asked himself, Why bother? it was unsettling. You ask yourself a question, you should try to answer.

"Isn't that trail to the sluice up here on the left?"

"Yeah," Billy nodded.

"Slow down. Let's take another look."

Billy slowed down and made the turn. The road led into heavy timber, and about one half-mile along they came to a fork. A small sign nailed to a large sycamore, painted on wood and about four foot high, pointed to the right and read "slews." Billy slowed, went over a couple of real bad pot holes; and took the road to the "slews."

At one point the road seemed to end at the edge of the

river valley, but then it dipped and swung left. Billy put the cruiser in a lower gear and braked down as he went through the switchbacks. They pulled up on an old logging trail, stopped, and walked down to the small, brown sandy beach.

"That's where I found the pouch," Billy pointed to the farthest end of the beach, where a tree had fallen and a bunch of weedy roots hung over the water.

The torrent was cascading and corkscrewing between the rocks, and McPhee judged the last fall to be about five feet into the pool. They couldn't see upriver, but at that moment the head of a paddler came into view about the sluice.

"Now that's where he came from," said Billy.

They watched as the paddler expertly and swiftly crossed the river almost at a right angle from the far shore. The current suddenly caught the front of the canoe, swinging it into rush of water that sluiced down between the rocks. The paddler dug in now. One, two, three strokes, driving the front of the canoe out high above the water in the middle of the torrent and then letting it fall at a forty-five-degree angle as he leaned way back to keep his balance. For a moment it seemed to hang, and then it dropped off towards the pool. The tail end of the canoe went under when it was hit by the torrent from above, but the paddler dug in hard on both sides and the canoe came free.

Both Billy and McPhee waved appreciatively at the paddler, who had swung left again with the course of the river, away from the falls and into the main current.

"Now there's a pro," said Billy.

"First rate."

They both felt a little exhilarated after watching the performance. At all times the man in the canoe had control. He had known enough to ferry across and approach the sluice at a right angle. He had built momentum to carry himself to the far rock, and when the swift current had swept the front of the canoe around, he had dug in again until it seemed he wanted to climb that rock, canoe and all. But he had known ahead of time that on this far side of the torrent, and by continually attacking the large rock to almost the point of turning over, he'd fly free of the center of the maelstrom below and escape the hydraulic.

Such hydraulics, where the water sets up a continuous roll at the bottom of the drop, have been known to hold people and canoes under for five or ten minutes without giving up their prey until it was too late. The experts understood this, and if the canoe filled and they had to get out, they'd go with the roll and find the current to carry then through. The amateurs tried to stay on top and fight their way out. Sometimes they did, but at other times there was trouble.

They both stared at the sluice.

"I figure he lost it just as he came in, and the current carried him left. He got a little crosswise and the canoe rolled as he went over. He probably got thrown towards those rocks." Billy indicated two or three jutting boulders to one side at the bottom of the sluice.

"Mm," said McPhee.

"Maybe he just didn't attack it. If you just let the canoe go along and don't attack it, you've had it most times."

They both studied the water. Then looked down at the brown sand. Billy's earlier footsteps were clearly visible, down to the water, over to the end of the beach where he'd found the pouch, and then straight back to the path.

There were a number of cuplike indentations in the sand going back to the path at regular intervals. McPhee squatted down and Billy did the same. They studied them in silence. Billy flicked a little sand away from one edge with his finger. They both followed the indentations back to the path with their eyes. The interval between the indentations seemed to match footprints here and there. At one point close to the water there seemed to be a larger hole, as if somebody had poured water out of a bucket.

"Not an animal, is it?" asked McPhee. He bowed to Billy's knowledge of the woods.

Billy shook his head. "Looks almost like water was poured on the ground in each place. It's just an idea. Doesn't mean anything at all. But if somebody didn't want to leave footprints, they'd bring a bucket and pour on a little water as they walked backward each step."

He was engrossed now, and was going through the motions of pouring water out of a bucket as he stepped backwards. He stopped as he reached the small outcrop of rock near the path.

"Tennis shoes, maybe, so the heel wouldn't dig in."

Billy went back to the car and returned with an empty coke can. He filled it with water and poured some next to three of the other spots. They looked the same.

They both stared at the brown sand in silence. The paddler and his canoe had disappeared around the bend. Except for the thunder of water, it was a peaceful place. The light glistened on the water, and a large pine overhung the pool and then had turned to grow straight up to catch the sun.

"Could have been somebody he knew," McPhee muttered almost to himself.

"Huh?" Billy was a short distance away, and the roar of the water was loud.

McPhee shook his head. "Nothing."

"You know, Pete, it must have been somebody he knew. Somebody who hollered to Jaynes. Jaynes came over in the canoe, put the prow on shore, took a couple of steps in the canoe, stepped out, and then bent over to pull the canoe up out of the river. When he bent over.

. . ." Billy stopped. He felt he was carrying it all just a little too far.

"You got that little Minolta in the car?"

Billy went back to the car to get it.

McPhee located the sun, and from about six feet away he took pictures of the series of indentations. Then he came in as close as he thought he could, adjusted the lens, and snapped some more of the indentations singly, then in twos, and then one of Billy pointing at the spot where they met the path. Actually, they didn't look like much, but he did get the pictures.

They poked around for another ten or fifteen minutes, taking a shot of where the packet was found and where the body had lodged. None of it seemed to make much sense, but they finished the roll. After all, people had drowned in the river before, and chances were there'd be more after this one.

Billy picked up a piece of a limb about the size of a baseball bat, and walking up the river he threw it directly under the torrent of water. It went under, bobbed to the surface, went under once more, and came up downriver. Then it slowly drifted into the current down past the spot where Billy had found the pouch, and around the bend. Both men just watched.

They both knew it didn't mean a thing. Even the little indentations in the sand, an animal, a bird, maybe a person was there. Yesterday, the day before. It wasn't evidence of anything.

As they crossed the bridge on the way back, they saw that the canoe was gone. They pulled up next to the Information Building, where the ranger was talking to four young folks gathered around him. He had a long chart of the river in one hand, and with the other he was pointing at the description of the sluice.

"See, right here it's designated as a Number VI. It says 'Danger! Danger! Danger!' three times." He looked earnestly at the young people. "Means exactly what it says." He went on reading. "For experts only. Do not attempt to navigate this area in a kayak or a canoe unless you are an expert. Strong hydraulic, high drop, and swift acceleration of water make this the most dangerous spot on the river. There is a portage on the right approximately fifty yards upriver."

His young listeners asked if they could have a chart.

"Sure, they're free."

At that moment the ranger saw McPhee. "Took the canoe up behind the building. And I got those tickets for you up through eleven o'clock. I thought that would be time enough. They're up at the office." He gave the young folks the chart and went off into the building.

McPhee said, "Let's take a look at the canoe."

They went around back and saw the canoe where it lay. It was bottom-side up. Just an ordinary, red fiberglass canoe with a hole in one end. McPhee took one end and Billy the other, and they turned it over. Two large chunks of foam, the extra flotation, and the life jacket were underneath.

McPhee bent over and ran his hand along the gunwale. Then he stopped.

Billy looked over and saw a dark brown smudge where McPhee's hand had stopped.

McPhee wiped his hand over it and looked at his finger. A little had come off.

"What is it?"

McPhee shook his head. "I don't know."

He took a paper from his pocket and, using Billy's jackknife, he scraped some of the brown stain into the center of the paper, folded it carefully, and gave it to Billy.

"Blood? Dried blood?"

McPhee looked at him. "Let's find out."

They both looked at what remained of the stain on the canoe.

"That's where his head would have been near when he got it, like it said."

"Mm." McPhee just didn't know.

"And when he got hit he could have bled a little, or it could have spurted."

"Well, if it is blood, I don't see how it got on the canoe if it was an accident."

Billy added, "He couldn't hang onto the canoe after he got hit because he'd be out cold. But we don't know."

"Right. Let's make certain that gets to the lab up in Asheville. On second thought, maybe we ought to take the canoe along with us."

"Where are you going to put it?"

McPhee thought about that. He pictured Billy and him carrying the thing into the county building.

"Why not take it over to my place? Put it in the shed around the back. Take the whole works." He indicated the foam and the jacket.

Billy nodded. "Right."

When they came around the front of the building, the ranger was waiting with a large, brown envelope. He handed it to McPhee. "Didn't know where you got to."

McPhee took the envelope. "Thanks. Billy will be by for the canoe."

As they walked back to the car, McPhee opened the envelope and began leafing through the tickets.

They got in, and Billy drove down to the parking lot and pulled up beside McPhee's car.

"Here's your boys, Billy. The guy you met and his pal." He showed Billy the ticket. "Stevens and Zybarski timed in at 7:35."

Billy nodded. "That's them."

"And here, 'Jaynes; time in, 7:20.' And look, take a look at this one."

He handed him the ticket and Billy read it out loud, "Spur Foss, 7:15."

They looked at one another. Spurgeon's boy. They'd

heard the rumors just like everybody else. That sort of stuff traveled fast. Among other things, Spur was a stud. The questions were obvious. Which pasture had the stud been in lately, and what was he doing on the river the same time as Jaynes? McPhee couldn't help but think of that tank top back at the big deck.

Billy stood for a minute. His mind was traveling the same route. "Well, I guess I'd better get back."

McPhee knew it was his decision, but he was not above getting opinions.

"I was thinking about an autopsy."

Billy lifted a shoulder. "So he drowned. What could you find out?"

"I don't know. That's why I'm thinking about it."

"Might raise a little hell."

"So?"

Billy kicked at a pebble. "So we might find out something."

"That's right."

After Billy left McPhee called on his car radio and told them he wanted an autopsy. He had the authority, and he used it.

8

The Agent

IT WAS MONDAY, the day after the drowning, and a certain amount of routine had pushed the second thoughts McPhee had about the accident to the back of his mind. "Domestics," as they called them, took up almost half of the time of his entire staff. Neighbors and dogs, husbands and wives, owners and renters, mothers and children—domestics covered all this and more. People wanted help from the sheriff's office. Even those social workers down the hall with eight people on nine to five, five days a week, wanted help from the sheriff's office. And here he had only twelve men on the road to cover the entire county, seven days a week, twenty-four hours a day.

Then about ten-thirty the hospital called. They said Mrs. Jaynes had identified the body. They also said she had told them to have the body sent to the Foss Funeral Home. When they told her about the autopsy, she had a fit. There was an old guy with her, and he had one too. The old guy called the judge at his home Sunday afternoon, and the judge said McPhee had the authority to do that, but he'd look into it. Then Mrs. Jaynes and the old fellow left. Still mad.

He asked if they found out anything, and they let him

talk to the medical examiner. He told McPhee the man drowned. Had a blow on the back of the head, probably rendered him unconscious, but the cause of death was drowning. Some lacerations on both knees. Everything else was normal. He'd send McPhee the full report when he finished. McPhee told him to let the body go when he was done. Foss Funeral Home, that was his understanding too.

He told Billy to go down and move the canoe over to his place and take a second look along the river, just in case. He'd sent out Lucas, his chief investigator, to check on Spur. See what he was doing running the river at 7:15.

He'd come back from lunch, checked through some reports they had on marijuana, and talked to them up in Ashville about when they'd get down with the helicopter to make an aerial survey. They told him the weather wasn't right and there was one job ahead of him, and maybe they'd give him a ring along about Thursday. He hung up.

It was raining. He wondered why he had ordered the autopsy. The man was running the river with no helmet, somehow he'd lost control going over the sluice, got a clunk on the head, and drowned. Billy and his bucket, footprints, how maybe the body couldn't have floated to where it was found without a good shove, was a fantasy. So anyway, he'd ordered it. A little solid investigation wouldn't hurt even though it was an accident. And he wondered about Spur.

He watched the rivulets form on the window and run down the pane, a little at a time, and then a big one all the way down. He watched the process repeat itself one more time, and his thoughts moved onto his wife. He was lonesome. He liked the dog, but on the nights when there wasn't much going on, it seemed a long ride out to the farm, and the quiet of it all was a little empty. Left him a little empty, too. And he didn't need all this. Things had been going along fine, up until now.

He heard the phone ring in the outer office. It rang again, and he waited for Mrs. Owens to answer. After the third ring, he picked it up himself. "Sheriff's office."

"Peter McPhee, please."

"This is Sheriff McPhee."

"McPhee, this is Hal Wainwright with the Atlanta office of the F.B.I. Is this a secure phone?"

McPhee looked out and saw that Mrs. Owens was still out. He wondered if it really was "secure." "Sure, go right ahead."

"Well, we've got an agent on the way up to see you, but I want the meeting to be strictly confidential. The agent is due to call in, and I wonder if we could arrange a meeting as soon as possible?"

"Did you say F.B.I.?"

"That's right. Now where can you meet?"

This stalled McPhee out. Then it blew his mind. Secure phones, F.B.I., confidential meeting! He looked at the rivulets on the window and leaned back in his chair.

"Well, what's it all about?"

"Rather not say over the phone, McPhee. Where can you meet Orsini?"

"Is this urgent?"

"Yes, it is, Sheriff."

McPhee ran his hand over his head. "And you don't want anybody to see us?"

"Right, and I don't want any of your people to know about it, either. And it may take a little time."

"Well, everybody knows me here, and this is a pretty small town. . . ."

"Yes." The voice was polite, authoritative, and just a little impatient.

"When's he going to be here?"

"Anytime after five, wherever you say."

This was the F.B.I. We better not blow it. "There's a new steak house, one of those modern places, on 347 on the way into town. 'Sizzlers,' the name. What if I drive through the parking lot at five-thirty. Tell him to follow me out."

"Fine, Sheriff. The Sizzler parking lot at five-thirty. Orsini will be driving a blue Skylark. Got it?"

"A blue Skylark. I got it. Oh, and Mr. Wainwright, how can I be sure this is on the level? I don't get calls from the F.B.I. every day."

"Good question, McPhee. Have you got an Atlanta phone book? Or better still, just call information. Give me a ring. F.B.I. central office in Atlanta. Just ask for Wainwright."

Five minutes later, after he'd confirmed the call, McPhee slumped back in his chair. The F.B.I. What in God's name did they want with him? He thought about what he had said, handled it pretty well, everything considered, especially that bit about the calling back. That was like a real pro. He sat there and looked at the rain on the window. The call had shaken him up, but he gradually settled back to normal. Then a thought struck him. What if the damn steak house was closed on Monday? A lot of them closed one day a week. He got out the phone book to look in the yellow pages for restaurants. It wasn't listed. Well, it was new. He called the operator, got the number, and dialed.

"Are you opcn today?"

A woman's voice told him they were open from eleven A.M. to ten-thirty at night. He hung up. What difference would it have made anyway, since he was just going through the parking lot? It would be better if it was open though, less conspicuous. He smiled to himself. He was always willing to admit it if he blew one. He just didn't like to do it too often.

He was doodling around the Atlanta phone number when Mrs. Owens came to the door.

"You look worried, Sheriff. Everything all right?"

"Fine, Mrs. Owens, just fine. What time is it?"

He ripped the number off his pad and threw it in the basket. The clock was right over the counter. He could see it from his chair. Mrs. Owens looked at it and then back at McPhee. Four-fifteen.

He turned in off the highway and noted that the restaurant parking lot was already half-full. He slowed down, made a complete swing of the lot and saw a blue Skylark at the end. It was still raining, but he could see that someone was in the front seat. As he came back to the entrance, he looked in the rearview mirror and saw that the Skylark had backed out and was now turning to follow. Out on the highway the car was still there, so he slowly accelerated up to about forty-five and headed out towards his farm. He knew of no other place in town where he could talk and not be seen or heard or surprised by someone. Off the highway with the blue car behind, three miles up into the cove, and then up the drive. The Skylark pulled up right behind him. Trees and bushes along the road blocked the view. They were safe here.

The dog was sitting on the porch as he drove in, and when the other car pulled in behind, he came barking to challenge the intruder.

McPhee got out of the car and put a reassuring hand on the dog's head. "Easy boy, we got company."

He walked back to the blue car and stopped. His head shifted gears in a hurry. He had been ready to put his best professional foot forward, welcome the agent to the county, and try to maintain an equal footing with what was probably one of Uncle Sam's finest. But this was different.

He stuck his head up closer to the driver. "You Orsini?"

She nodded, and her shoulder-length, black, wavy hair moved back and forth around a face with warm dark eyes. She smiled at him. "Surprised?"

"A little, I guess."

He opened the door for her, and Brook came over to check out the visitor.

She got out of the car in three easy motions, each one better than the first, and both he and Brook watched admiringly.

"What a beautiful Brittany." She stopped to scratch the dog's head. "What's his name?"

McPhee had seen a leggy young doe one time, and it moved the same way and had the same warm, wary eyes. No nonsense here, though. She'd taken in the sex and the breed all with one glance.

"Brook."

At the mention of his name, the dog looked up at him. He was enjoying the attention, and it showed all over his face. McPhee thought he probably looked the same way the dog did.

"You named him 'Brook' because he's bright, sparkling, and runs well, like a brook?"

McPhee laughed. "You've got it. Good downhill dog."

She smiled at that, too, and reached into the front seat and came up with a black briefcase.

"Can I help?"

She shook her head and followed him onto the front porch. He unlocked the door and let her go ahead. She laid the briefcase on the coffee table in front of the fireplace and looked around appraisingly. "Nice. Comfortable looking."

"Would you like a drink? Coke, coffee, a beer, something a little stronger?"

"Coffee will be fine. Instant's okay, too."

McPhee went into the kitchen, put the kettle on, got out two cups, jar of coffee, Cremora, and noted he was humming to himself.

Now just a minute, McPhee. He laid the spoon on the counter. This is an agent of the federal government in your living room. She's a nice-looking lady, but let's keep our feet right on the ground where they belong. He stopped humming and measured the coffee carefully into the two cups.

"Orsini, uh . . . ?" He moved a little towards the archway so he could see her.

"Yes?"

"Is it Miss or Mrs.?"

"Maria will be fine, and I'm single."

"Well, I was going to ask whether you took sugar or cream?"

"Just a little cream, please."

When he brought in the coffee she was looking at his books on either side of the fireplace, reading the titles, too. She looked over her shoulder. "You like to read." It was a statement.

"I used to read a lot, but then I got busy and well, you know how it is."

She turned back and went on looking at the books.

He set one coffee next to the briefcase in front of the couch and put his own on the lamp table next to his chair. Then he went back to the kitchen for napkins. On second thought, he grabbed a box of chocolate chip cookies and came back into the living room.

"Herman Melville, Mark Twain, Joseph Conrad, and oh, I had to read that one at the F.B.I. Academy." She pointed to the book. He moved closer and saw that it was *Games People Play*. She stood up, and McPhee became very conscious of the closeness of her. It was a warmth tinged with just a faint trace of one of those spicy perfumes. They both stood there for a moment, not moving. Then the dog nudged the box of cookies with his nose.

"Wife's been gone a long time, eh, McPhee?"

He nodded, cleared his throat, sat down, and put the box of cookies on the coffee table next to the briefcase.

"You do your homework well."

"We always like to know what we're getting into." She took off the beige jacket and laid it on the back of the couch. Then she moved over to the end of the couch near his chair, sat down, and lit a cigarette.

"Why don't you tell me about what happened to Jay Jay Jaynes so we can see what we've got so far." Her voice was soft now, but businesslike. It had lost most of its enthusiasm and taken on a quiet directness. She spooned a little Cremora into the coffee, took a sip, and looked at him with those wary doe-eyes.

McPhee looked down at his shoes. They were grubby and wet. He had to admit she was good. She'd taken him a little on his blind side, eased through all the defenses, warmed him up a little, cooled him down, and taken charge, as it were. Now for the business at hand.

He reached over, got a cookie, and gave it to the dog. He didn't know why, but he felt like a teenager about to tell his mother how he'd wrecked the car.

"Something wrong, McPhee?"

"No. I was just thinking that those people that work in personnel at the F.B.I sure know what they're doing."

"Well, it's not easy, meeting a man in a parking lot, following him home, and then finding that he's a gentleman as well as a pro."

She smiled at him, just a pleasant smile this time. McPhee felt a little better.

"Jaynes was a big man in defense electronics. For the time being, let's just say that we're interested."

He told her the whole story then. About Billy finding the canoe and the body, about the two fellows from

Atlanta, about Spur, and about his visit to the Jaynes home. How he'd met Gloria Jaynes, Lochmiller, and the Bradhams. He didn't mention his ordering an autopsy, and he didn't mention Billy's thoughts about the possible footprints and the bucket and the stain on the canoe. After all, that was next to nothing.

"Now, you say he did have a life jacket but no helmet?"

"That's right. And the canoe had a hole in it, and there was some kind of an abrasion on the back of his head."

"Is the river high now?"

"Sure. Always higher in the spring."

"And that makes it more dangerous. I suppose others have lost their lives that way?"

"There's been about half a dozen that I remember over the past maybe five or six years."

"So, what do you make of it all, McPhee?"

"I think it was an accident."

"Then why did you order the autopsy?"

McPhee stood up and went into the kitchen to get the kettle and coffee. She let him tell the whole story, yet she probably knew it by heart. He came back and set the kettle and coffee on the table in front of her.

"Now, suppose you tell me why all this cloak and dagger approach, and why I've got a lady F.B.I. agent in my living room."

She spooned out the coffee and added hot water. "Could I have a little cream, please?"

He got her the Cremora.

While he was gone she'd opened the briefcase and was making notes. She put the pad down, selected a folder from the briefcase, and placed it in front of her.

"You know anything about computers, chips, bits, microprocessors?"

"A little. Try me."

"Silicon Valley?"

"It's out near San Francisco where they make a lot of that stuff."

"Very good, McPhee. Ten or twelve years ago Jaynes, this same fellow who drowned, was one of the wonder boys out in Silicon Valley. He was with an outfit called Bowman Bassett. They helped develop the 64K RAM chip. This chip was four times as powerful as the one already on the market, the16K RAM. You follow?"

"It could handle more information?"

"Exactly. Something like 64,000 bits as opposed to 16,000. Then they went ahead and speeded up the time element to the point where the processing of the information was drastically cut."

Orsini paused and lit another cigarette.

McPhee noted that it was only her second.

"These things are vital to our defense establishment. The F.B.I., as well as other government agencies, try to keep track of all these new developments, as well as the people involved. And it's not easy."

"I can appreciate that." Then he added, "But that's what they get paid to do," and he felt better.

She put the cigarette down and clasped her hands in front of her.

"Jaynes was a wonder boy. He founded Contel, and the stock in the company went from a few million to over two hundred million in a period of a year or two. Jaynes turned out to be a big promoter. Contel grew with him. He wheeled and dealed and got to be a real heavyweight, defense contracts and all. When a real heavyweight with defense contracts has an accident, we want the details. They are big people, McPhee, and they live in your backyard."

McPhee sat slumped in his chair.

"Why bother with me? Why not move in and take over? After all, I've only had the job for three months."

"Time on the job doesn't necessarily mean a thing,

McPhee. We had an agent with us for thirty years who wound up in bed with a Russian blonde. You probably read about it."

He had. It had happened out in Washington or Oregon somewhere.

"It boils down to whom we trust. Before Webster came in as the new head of the F.B.I. it was like a sieve. An American firm would make a new product, sell it overseas, and it would be resold to the Russians in a matter of weeks. In the last two years it's been much better. We have people in all the real sensitive plants, some undercover and some right on top. We're doing much, much better."

McPhee waited. When Maria didn't say anything else, he asked, "You have people in this plant?"

"Of course." She took a sip of her coffee. "As a matter of fact, we have reason to suspect that somebody here has been selling to the Russians. We don't know who it is but from what our overseas people have told us, we're sure it comes from here. As a matter of fact, we thought something was going to take place over the weekend. We had quite a setup here, waiting for whoever it was to make their move. Instead, we have an accident."

McPhee got up and wandered around the room. He looked at the clock on the mantle, the books, the stereo, but he didn't see much of anything. Finally, he turned around.

"So?"

"When an accident happens, someone should look into it, right?"

"Right."

"Well, if no one made a move over the weekend, and it was an accident, we see no reason why they shouldn't try again, maybe in a day or two, or a week or two."

"Unless it was Jay Jay."

"Unless it was Jay Jay. You're the man, McPhee. You're the logical one to investigate the accident. If we got into it, we'd blow our cover and a year's work would go down the drain. Wainwright told me to use my own judgment about talking to you. There are a lot of different kinds of sheriffs. I'm telling you all I can."

"I suppose I should thank you, but along about now I think I should have stayed with insurance."

She smiled, and he sat down again.

"Instead of a move, we get an accident."

"So you want me to go ahead . . . on this accident?"

"That's right."

"How do you know that maybe the C.I.A. or even the Russians didn't kill Jay Jay?"

"We don't."

"But you want me to find out?"

"Not really, McPhee, not really at all. You just do your regular thing. Ask around, talk to these people. If you get suspicious, push a little. But you already told me you thought it was an accident."

He wondered if he should tell her about Billy and those footprints and the stain on the canoe, and thought better of it. After all, if it was an accident, he was home free. Better to wait and see how things come along.

"Just keep us informed of any developments you think we should know about. And, McPhee," she waited until she had his eyes, "no one but yourself is to know what I've told you, or know that I've been here."

McPhee considered what she said.

"Just supposing it wasn't an accident. You think it might be the same person, the one that's selling and the one that killed Jay Jay?"

"That's pure conjecture, McPhee. We simply don't know. Just do your thing and keep in touch."

She put a card on the table. "That's a special phone number where you can reach me at any time." The number was written on the back.

She opened the briefcase and took out four files.

"You probably should have these as well, but keep them at home. Don't bring them to the office or leave them in your car: Jay Jay, Lochmiller, Bradham, and Gloria. You've met Gloria."

"Ah, yes."

"She's no dumb blond, McPhee—Magna cum laude, Pembroke, a good school, the woman's Ivy League. . . ."

He looked at the files.

"Okay."

She began gathering her things.

McPhee nodded and thought about Billy again and the stain on the canoe.

"Okay."

"So be it." She closed the briefcase.

The dog came over and she scratched its head. It was quiet in the room, and just a little colder. They heard the sound of a jet far overhead.

"Atlanta to Washington, about this time every night," said McPhee.

Maria stood up, brushed the wrinkles out of her skirt, and picked up the jacket off the back of the couch. She looked at the walnut clock on the mantle. It was eight forty-five.

McPhee was still fingering the files on the table.

"You'll be back?"

"I'll be back in two, maybe three days. Give you a little time to sort it out."

"Hmm." McPhee patted the dog's head and contemplated his shoes.

"What is it?"

"Well, I thought it might be a little easier for both of us if we had dinner here next time. I'm not a bad cook. How does the F.B.I. feel about such things?"

"Well, I'll check with Wainwright, but so far as the hired help goes, I think the F.B.I. would take kindly to the idea."

They went out into the cool mountain air and walked slowly to her car. He opened the door and she got in.

"What's the best time to call?" She looked at him and held his eyes.

"I'm always in around four-thirty."

"I'll call."

He nodded and waved as she turned the car and drove away. He watched the headlights down the road and then looked up at the stars. The dog came over and nosed his leg.

"She's quite a gal, F.B.I."

The dog seemed unimpressed. McPhee watched him as he went over and left his mark on the apple tree.

Then he went back into the house, sank down in the chair, and looked at the folders she'd left.

He picked up the first one. "Lochmiller" on the top, followed by a number, six digits. He opened it and read through the basic information. Fifty-eight years old, some university in Europe he couldn't pronounce, executive vice president of Lumeniere, eight years on the job, major stockholder, company moved into prominent position in electronics four years ago. Does business in South America, Europe, and North America, as well as East Germany and Poland and Rumania. McPhee wondered what that meant. Was that why the F.B.I. was on his doorstep?

He picked up the one on Jaynes. Forty-four years old, University of North Carolina, electrical engineering, graduate work at Stanford, Palo Alto. Bowman Bassett in Silicon Valley, founded Contel, came in with Lumeniere eight years ago. McPhee checked the dates. Some dates. Lochmiller probably brought him in. Vice president for North American operations and he was making $478,000 a year. Lot of money. He checked Lochmiller's file again. No salary given. He noted Jaynes had been divorced twice, so Gloria was his third try.

Bradham. Virginia Tech, electrical engineering, Bowman Bassett, and then to Contel, same date as Jaynes. Jaynes must have known him for some time. Manager, Bryson County Plant and making $72,000. Not bad, but not in thc samc lcague as Jaynes.

He spread them all out in front of him and leafed through them one more time. Lochmiller liked stamps and women. Jaynes liked skiing, golf and canoeing. Bradham, flying and golf.

Not much on any of them. They'd told him just what they wanted him to know, no more, no less. 'If it was an accident, McPhee, and we hope it was, forget it. If it's more than that, we'll help a little, but keep us informed.' And they send a woman agent to keep track of him, a Maria, a woman.

McPhee closed the folders, put them in a neat stack in the middle of the coffee table, and went to bed. The dog followed him into the bedroom and curled up in his spot next to the dresser.

But McPhee lay there looking into the darkness, listening to the sounds of the night. What if he did find out it was murder? What did he have to go on, especially in that league? He could be trading a nice, cozy, closed case for a lot of egg on his face. Maybe the F.B.I. was a little smarter than he was. He let his mind linger on that for a while and decided he just didn't want to be that smart.

And then he thought about Maria, and that didn't help much, either. The dog whined and let out a few light barks. Something was bothering him too, in a dream.

"It's okay boy, it's all right." He said it out loud so the dog would hear. He listened, and the dog made no further noise.

McPhee rolled over on his back and folded his hands on his chest. Somewhere he'd read that this was the regal position for sleep. He smiled to himself and was gone.

9

The Team

IT WAS TUESDAY morning, nine o'clock. McPhee had told Billy and Lucas to meet with him at ten in his office. He sat at his desk and looked at the papers arranged on its top. He had the medical report and the small stack of "put in" tickets. Next to them was a one-page report Lucas had typed up on Spur. Then there were the pictures they had taken of the marks in the sand, and he also had some notes on Jay Jay, his wife Gloria, Lochmiller, and Bradham. He had copied them off the profiles. Squarely in front of him was the report from Asheville. It stated that the stain was human blood, the same rare type as Jaynes, AB negative, and it had not been on the canoe for over twenty-four hours. McPhee sat there tapping the end of his pencil on the desk. He tried to think of a logical explanation of how the blood got on the canoe. Every time he tried to be objective, the picture of Billy came back to him acting it out—pouring the water to erase the footprints, calling Jaynes over to that little brown beach. When Jaynes bent over to pull up the canoe, somebody knocked him in the head. And a little blood got on the canoe.

His phone buzzed. Mrs. Watson told him it was Judge Carpenter. He'd been expecting this one.

"Mornin', Judge."

He heard the genial but sharp-edged voice on the other end.

"How's everything at the sheriff's office, McPhee?"

"Fine, just fine, Judge." He waited.

"McPhee, I had a call from a fella by the name of Lochmiller, with that electronics plant. He was with Mrs. Jaynes, and they had a question about the autopsy. Why did you order it, McPhee?"

McPhee told him that the man had been an expert, been down the river many times, this time without a helmet, and he told him about the bloodstain. He didn't mention Spur or the fellow from Atlanta, or how the body wasn't found near the pouch, or how Billy's stick floated on down past them both. He just stopped after the bloodstain bit.

There was a silence on the other end of the line. McPhee waited.

"He could have cut his finger, sliver, or something."

"He could have, Judge."

"Well, these are pretty big people, McPhee. I understand they even have defense contracts down there."

McPhee knew that, but he could still see no sense in saying anything more, so he didn't.

"McPhee, you still there?"

"Yes, sir."

"Well, I just thought I'd call and let you know. A little investigation can't do any harm. If it's an accident, it's an accident. As they say, McPhee, if it ain't broke, don't fix it, right?"

"Right, Judge."

"These are fine people. Let's not make a mess if we don't have to. I'll see you."

He hung up, and so did McPhee.

McPhee picked up the report from Lucas, his chief investigator. Lucas had typed "Just wooden talk."

McPhee didn't see a great deal wrong with it except the spelling. The meaning was very clear.

Lucas was a good ole boy. He had been with the department longer than anyone else. Perhaps he couldn't spell, but give him an expense report and it better be right. Or let them try to fiddle a little on the cruiser maintenance over at the garage, Lucas wanted to see the parts, worn or broken.

When McPhee was elected, he'd chosen Billy as his chief deputy because Billy was good with the men—easy, quiet, willing to do more than his share to keep things going well. In order not to bend Lucas's nose, McPhee had given him the title of chief investigator and also had him handle maintenance and finances. He got along well with Mrs. Watson, who did most of the bookkeeping, and it worked out fine.

Lucas and Billy were waiting outside. He motioned them in.

Lucas was a big man, big like an ox. He was well over six feet and weighed over two hundred and fifty pounds. He could move well, and had a small farm that kept him in shape. If he'd been born thirty years later, he probably would have been a millionaire by now after serving his time with the Green Bay Packers or the Washington Redskins. Even his feet were big, thirteen triple E. He had three sons, and the high school football coach knew them all by their first names before they were in the sixth grade. It was said that they literally filled one another's shoes. All three wore thirteen triple E, and the boys were spaced out nicely, two and three years apart.

Lucas came in, fitted his bulk into the chair, and eased down on it. The chair held. Billy closed the door and sat opposite Lucas.

"You get my report on Spur?" Lucas asked.

McPhee picked it up from his desk.

"I don't know what's the matter with that boy. He said he made out the ticket, put it in the box, and then decided not to go. After that he just wooden talk."

McPhee noted that from a phonetic point of view, his spelling had been correct.

"Was Foss there?"

"Sure, we both were. But the kid got mad and finally walked out."

He used the word "kid" even though Spur was in his middle twenties. "Course, it don't mean anything. Spur's a good kid, a little wild, maybe. You know what the talk has been."

He looked at McPhee and Billy in turn. He fit his little finger into his ear, dug at it, and then pulled the finger out and examined the tip. Billy noted that there was nothing there.

"There's some talk goin' round that Spur was havin' it on with this Mrs. Jaynes. Martha told me." Martha was his wife, the mother of his three sons.

Billy and McPhee had heard rumors, but a source such as Martha carried substance. While they thought about this, with its possible implications, Lucas took out a wooden match and inserted the end into his ear, twirling it between his thumb and forefinger. Billy had seen him do it before, and he always expected Lucas to drill a hole in his head. Lucas took the match out, wiped it clean with his finger, and put it back in his pocket.

"It don't necessarily mean a thing. You know Foss, his daddy, comes down on him pretty hard, and Spur is different. Hell, you got a whole handful of people around that river about that time,"—he indicated the "put in" slips on McPhee's desk—"and that don't mean much either."

"Lucas, I want to talk to Spur, and the sooner the better."

"He's not here anymore."

McPhee shot him a look. "What do you mean he's not here anymore?"

"Foss called me this mornin'. He took off."

"Well, where did he go?"

Lucas looked at the floor. "That's why he called me. He don't know."

"Well, you find him, Lucas. You find him. Even if it takes a warrant and an all points with the state police, you find that kid and get him back here."

McPhee found himself getting real involved. After all, Lucas didn't know it was shaping up into a murder investigation. He didn't want to sound jumpy. Lucas was a good man. He settled back.

"Can you do that all right?"

Lucas had felt the heat, and he was still looking at the floor. "Yeah. I'll find him."

"Do you need any help?"

"No, I'll find him by myself." He gave McPhee a stony man-to-man, dead-or-alive look, and McPhee believed him. He guessed he'd better get on with it.

"You know the stain we found on the canoe?"

Both of them looked at him expectantly.

"It was blood, same type as Jaynes's. And it wasn't old."

They all digested this fact. Lucas broke the silence.

"Could've cut his finger." He looked straight at McPhee as if daring him to deny it.

McPhee, after hearing the same thing from the judge, said, "Could have, but we've got a number of little things as well."

They all went over what they had. The washed-out footprints, the fact that Jaynes was an expert, no helmet although he usually wore one, even the stick that floated on by the pouch and the body. He even gave them a rundown on the profiles he had of Jay Jay, Mrs. Jaynes,

Lochmiller, and Bradham. Said he got them from someone he knew at the plant.

"So where does that leave us?"

McPhee had a pretty fair idea himself, but he wanted Lucas and Billy with him.

Billy tilted his chair back a little.

"Why would anybody want to kill him?"

Lucas brought it up. "I heard they had defense contracts down there." He said it matter-of-factly. "No tellin' what's goin' on."

McPhee nodded thoughtfully and noted that this could put Spur in the clear.

Billy brought his chair back down.

"What about those fellows from Atlanta? We ought to check them out for sure."

"You want to go? There's a guy I used to know with the Atlanta police by the name of Curtis, a detective. You want to go?"

Billy thought of Julie complaining. It would mean leaving her alone. He had an idea.

"If I pay her way, can I take Julie?"

McPhee looked at him. "You think she'd want to go?"

"Sure. The boy could stay with his grandmother. Take my own car if you give me mileage."

McPhee looked at Lucas. He didn't want to start anything. This was expense-account business.

Lucas said, "We've got the one cruiser out on transmission."

Whenever a car was being repaired, it was always "out," according to Lucas. Out on brakes, out on carburetor, or out on bodywork. Whatever, it was "out."

"I'll call Harris and see if he can get with you tomorrow. I'll let you know. And Lucas, set me up with Spur and Foss, either at his house or at the funeral home. Make it early. And see what else you can find out from some of the folks, Lucas. We must have a lot of people working down around those places in the valley. Maybe the Jaynes have a maid?"

Lucas looked at the floor.

"You really think somebody killed this guy?"

Billy spoke up, "I do. I think so."

Lucas looked at McPhee.

But McPhee shook his head.

"I don't know. I just don't know. But it's our job to find out."

10

The Mourners

McPHEE DIDN'T LOOK forward to this visit. He turned off the highway into the entrance of Emerald Valley. At the gate house the security man asked if he had an appointment. McPhee showed his badge and said that he planned to look around. The security man asked if there was someone he could call. McPhee said, "no," and looked at him. Then the security guard let him through.

The entry road was six lanes of black asphalt, three on each side. In between the lanes was an island of flowers. On each side of the road, all the underbrush had been cleared and as far as the eye could see there was rich, lush, close-cut green grass. The larger trees had been left standing. Those close to the road were encircled with flowers. Further away, each tree had a perimeter of bark mulch at its base. And all the trees were set in this green sea of smooth grass, Emerald Valley. Jay Jay had known what he was doing.

In wide, sweeping curves the road wound up at the base of the mountain. A caution light signaled the first cutoff road. The sign read To the Complex. The next was To the Stables, while a third was To the Lift and a fourth To the Villas. After that the roads were given names such as Quail Run, Bear Hollow, and Fox Chase. Patches of forest were left standing here and there to give privacy to the homes. Fifty thousand dollars for a half-acre lot to qualified buyers. McPhee was impressed—not overwhelmed or intimidated, just impressed.

He heard the stereo as he pulled up in the drive. When he pressed the doorbell, the stereo stopped and the dog began barking. Someone told the dog to be quiet and the barking stopped.

Gloria Jaynes opened the door. She stood there looking at him, the dog to one side. Her head was wrapped in a white turban, and the dark blue wrap-around hung in full folds to the floor. It was gathered at the waist with a sash, and the neckline dropped with a plunging "v" all the way to the sash. She pulled at the top of the gown as her poise returned, and that distant look seemed to hold him off.

"What is it, McPhee?"

"I want to talk to you about your husband's death."

"Is this an official visit?"

McPhee smiled. It was a boyish smile, and it took almost ten years off his grand total of twenty-nine. It always got him in, even when he was selling insurance.

"Just about all my visits are official."

"Come in, please." She led him into the large, beamed living room with the glass doors on one side leading to the deck, sat in a wing chair near the end of the couch, and motioned him to the corner of the couch about six feet away.

"Would you care for anything?"

He shook his head. There was an awkward silence, and Gloria crossed those long, beautiful legs and adjusted the folds at the knee. The adjustment still left him a little thigh. He looked into those faraway eyes.

"I wanted to explain about the autopsy."

Her lips tightened.

"Both Locky—Mr. Lochmiller—and I thought it completely unwarranted."

"Well, it's just part of our routine when a death occurs in somewhat strange circumstances."

"What was so strange? He neglected to wear his helmet, and he paid for his poor judgment."

McPhee thought of Billy. She was a cold one.

"Well, he was an expert, and he'd run the river many times before, and he did get quite a blow on the head."

"I thought that was obvious."

"The medical examiner said it knocked him unconscious and he drowned." He leaned forward on the couch and spread his hands in front of him. "Now the only thing I'm trying to do is confirm the fact that this was an accident. But I do need a little more information."

She looked at him appraisingly and waited.

"Did anyone ever find the helmet?"

"It was in the back of the pickup, the other one. We have two. I have no idea how it got there, and neither does Locky. Do you want to fingerprint it or something? If so, I should tell you we both handled it. Looked it over and put it back."

"When did you find it?"

"Yesterday morning, when we looked for it."

So much for the helmet.

"Mr. Lochmiller drove him over?"

"Yes, he did. Said he got lost on the way back."

McPhee wasn't sure if he detected the flicker of a smile, not in the eyes, just the mouth.

"Were you here when he returned?"

"This is beginning to sound like a police interrogation, Sheriff. If you don't mind, I'm going to have a drink. Will you join me?"

McPhee thought about it.

"I'll have a Coke, or whatever."

She went over to a bar behind McPhee, and he heard her dropping the ice in the glass. He looked at the dog, and the dog seemed amused by it all.

"As a matter of fact, I always go jogging on Sunday morning, Sundays and Wednesdays, rain or shine. Although I won't go tomorrow because of the funeral. I'll go Thursday instead this week. I didn't get back until after Locky had returned. I don't know how long he'd been back."

She handed him the Coke and a napkin and sat down opposite him again, recrossing those long legs, sipping her drink, and looking at him over the glass. McPhee couldn't help but observe that the long gown was once again badly in need of adjustment. Gloria seemed not to notice.

"Mrs. Jaynes, was there anyone who would benefit, or who would really want to see your husband dead?"

He had a difficult time with the question, and he looked at her earnestly.

"I take it you don't do this sort of thing very often, McPhee. Do you?"

She seemed to be enjoying herself in a grim sort of way, and McPhee thought about Spur and wished she'd rearrange that skirt over that thigh so he wouldn't be distracted.

"Well, I ask a lot of questions in my work. It goes with the job."

"McPhee, any number of people might, as you say, 'benefit.' Actually, the insurance alone will probably keep me very comfortable for the rest of my life. In the world of electronics and corporate finance, however, you don't move the way Jay Jay did without stepping over dead bodies. And McPhee, if you're wondering why there are no widow's tears, Jay Jay and I left that part of our arrangement behind us years ago. We were . . . up until Sunday, a convenience to one another, nothing more."

McPhee looked and listened and watched her as she got up and went over to refill her glass. Somehow, he was glad that Billy was not here. She sounded almost as if she could have killed Jaynes herself.

She came back, sat down, and McPhee looked out at the mountains behind her.

"As a matter of fact, Locky was afraid of Jay Jay. I think he was probably relieved by the accident. Locky was the old lion at the top of the heap, and Jay Jay was about to drag him down. Jay Jay was poised for the kill. And there were others."

"Why should you tell me about Lochmiller?"

"It's no secret, Sheriff. Actually it was in *Business Week* a few days ago. Just trying to save you a little time so you can close this case and be done with it. Contel stock dropped twelve points as soon as the market opened yesterday. Today's not much better. A large part of my inheritance will be in that stock, McPhee."

She seemed to have lost that faraway look for the moment, and she was looking at him matter-of-factly now, coldly, but with a little curiosity.

"What did you do before you were a sheriff, McPhee?"

"Sold insurance in Atlanta."

"Why'd you come back here?"

"My father died."

There was a silence in the room. Gloria turned and looked at the mountains. She got up, walked to the glass door, slid it back, and let the dog out onto the deck. She was a big woman, capable, cold, and confident. He tried to picture her in Billy's place, with the bucket, or the rock, or holding the body under the water. She said they were a "convenience" to one another. And what happened when it became inconvenient?

"Is there anything else, Sheriff?"

McPhee put his empty glass on the table and got up.

"No, no. Thank you, Mrs. Jaynes. You've been very helpful."

"Sometimes, Sheriff, accidents can be strange. But they are still accidents."

She showed him to the door.

As he drove back to the highway, the grass just didn't seem so green on both sides of the street in Emerald Valley.

As he was leaving, Gloria had told him that Locky was playing golf, so McPhee turned off "To the Complex" and found the restaurant, which had a terrace overlooking the ninth and eighteenth greens.

Lochmiller was by himself on the terrace under a large, yellow and white umbrella.

"Mr. Lochmiller, I'm Sheriff McPhee. Mind if I sit down?"

"I remember. The sheriff, the young sheriff." He shook his lionlike head. "Autopsy. Why not sit down. Will you join me in a beer?" Without waiting for an answer, he called the waiter over.

"You want a Heineken too? It's really the only beer in this country that tastes the way a beer should taste." He noted the hesitation on McPhee's part. "On duty? You worried somebody will see you?"

McPhee shook his head and smiled.

"I'll have a light, draft if you've got it."

"Miller?"

"Fine."

After they'd settled in with the beer, Lochmiller leaned back appraisingly.

"So what's on your mind, Sheriff, Jay Jay and the river? The autopsy told you it was poison after all, eh?"

McPhee grinned.

"I wondered if you were satisfied that it was an accident?"

"Why not?" He had taken a huge pipe from his pocket and was carefully packing it from a yellow pouch.

"Why not?" he repeated. "A man, impulsive man in

many ways, goes down a wild river in a canoe, no helmet, and the water is high. So he gets a knock on the head and that's that. It's an accident. What could be simpler?"

Locky had had a few. McPhee wondered just how many.

"So you're worried about the helmet? We both looked in the back of the truck. He says, 'I always leave it from the last time, it should be here.' But it's not. I even told him, don't go. The rule says nobody goes, but he goes anyway."

"Did you look for it thoroughly?"

"Certainly. We both did, but it wasn't there. It's not a big truck. You can see all around. It just wasn't there."

He spoke with a slight accent, and McPhee was somewhat impressed with the candid account. He recognized the seemingly open-handed logic, and couldn't tell whether it was the simple truth or an expression of over-confidence helped along by a few beers and a young sheriff. If so, he liked the touch of Lochmiller helping to look for the helmet.

"I understand the helmet's been found?"

"Gloria told you, eh?"

He took a second look at McPhee.

"We found it yesterday, in the other truck. Who knows?"

McPhee looked at a foursome that was finishing up on the eighteenth. The guy missed a two-foot putt.

"It's just that he was an expert. And he'd run the river so often. Seems a little strange."

Lochmiller regarded him good-naturedly, with not a little condescension.

"Strange? You trying to make a murder, McPhee?"

He seemed to regard McPhee in a different light.

McPhee smiled. "No, not really. I just don't want to lay it to rest until I'm sure it's dead."

Lochmiller shrugged. "Young people, they never want to leave well enough alone. They don't know so much."

He considered this mild insult to be enough for the present and began to light his pipe with a gold lighter that had been lying on the table next to the pouch. He drew the flame into the bowl and let out large clouds of smoke. Then he seemed to be examining the lighter.

McPhee sat silent.

"You know about our company, Lumeniere and Contel?"

"A little."

"We are a big company, Sheriff. We have over thirty million in defense contracts alone. Thirty million. If we thought somebody killed Jay Jay, we could have an army in here tomorrow if we wanted to. The governor of your state, McPhee, he'd be glad to come down and help. So why should you worry yourself, you a . . . ?"

"A sheriff," McPhee charitably filled in the blank, "with a small county."

Lochmiller continued. "How could somebody do something like that? The man was on a river. If they wanted to kill him, shoot him in the head."

Lochmiller considered this for a moment and it sounded pretty good. But on second thought he added. "Unless they wanted to make it look like an accident. Hmm?"

"That's right."

"So who could have done it?"

He looked at the sheriff.

"You don't think me?" He was grinning.

"I don't think anyone. I'm just trying to confirm the fact that it was an accident."

Lochmiller seemed to be enjoying himself.

"So I drove him over, or I went with him. He drove. It was a trip, too, fog and all. We couldn't find the helmet so he went anyway. I got lost on the way back. I could have used the time to kill him and just said I was lost, eh?"

McPhee just looked at his beer. The man was playing with him.

"So you ask me where I got lost, and I'll tell you 'lost is lost.' It doesn't know where, that's what I tell you."

He seemed pleased with this explanation, and he smiled at McPhee and drank some beer.

"Let me help you, Mr. Sheriff. If I wanted to get rid of Jay Jay, I would probably pay somebody to do it. You know what it takes in this country?"

He looked at McPhee.

"It's cheaper here than in Europe. Five thousand dollars and my worries are over, five thousand dollars."

McPhee looked out over the terrace to the golf course. He thought about this, and wondered about that fellow on the river who was from Atlanta.

"Were you sorry it happened?"

Lochmiller looked at him in dismay. He seemed struck with the thought. McPhee couldn't tell whether it was a splendid performance or an honest reaction.

"Of course I was sorry. He was one of our top-notch men. What kind of a question is that?"

McPhee held his gaze steady out on the terrace onto the golf course and kept quiet. The other man sat back and looked at him knowingly.

"Gloria again. But it's no secret. It's true. He was young, like you, Sheriff. He wanted to change things, and he talked to some of our board, big stockholders, but only one or two. Why should I deny it? It makes things easier for me now that he's gone. But kill him, no, never!"

He shook his head firmly in self-affirmation and lifted his glass.

"Were there people that did hate him that much?"

Lochmiller seemed reluctant to stop playing the part of the elder adviser.

"Well, you didn't know Jay Jay. He was like a computer in some ways. His head was always ticking, never stopped. And always moving—goals, goals, goals, short-term, long-term—everybody had to have goals. He had a goal, too, but see what happened? He was too pushy and he forgot his helmet. That's what happened. He was too pushy, McPhee, too pushy." His eyes looked shrewdly and knowingly. "You know that kind of a man?"

McPhee wasn't sure whether it was a threat or whether he was still describing Jay Jay.

"These men are different. They make enemies. They don't think they are like other people."

"Until they forget their helmet."

"Good, McPhee."

Lochmiller looked at him as if seeing him in another light, and his eyes narrowed a little. There was a pause. He learned over and tapped McPhee on the arm.

McPhee didn't move the arm, but he turned to look. He saw Lochmiller's eyes now, tired but shrewd eyes that had seen and survived many battles.

"Believe me, young man, it was an accident, an accident. Rest assured. We are a big company, we know."

He patted McPhee's arm again, and McPhee nodded as if in agreement. But Lochmiller had talked too much, and both of them knew it.

The sign read Skeenah Valley Road. He remembered it from earlier days when it was just a one-way dirt track with weeds and brush almost meeting in the center and a rickety bridge about a mile up the creek. The road was well paved now, with a newly painted center line, and the bridge could easily handle the eighteen-wheelers that moved in and out. An eight-foot chain link fence with three strands of barbed wire at the top ran parallel to the road about twenty feet back. Floodlights, and what he knew to be TV cameras, were placed strategically at about two-hundred-foot intervals. Driving along the highway at night, it was lit up like the local high school football stadium, but these lights burned seven nights a week instead of just on Friday.

He drove through the entrance gate and by a small, empty guardhouse, evidently not manned during daylight hours. At a sign that read Visitor Parking he turned in and pulled up at an angle away from the building. He noticed that those parking slots closest to the front entrance had small identification signs. The closest one said Mr. Jaynes and the next one Mr. Bradham. There were five or six more, but cars were parked in them, a Mercedes, Cadillac, Porsche, and he couldn't tell the rest. But no car in the spot reserved for Jaynes.

The building was long, one-story, red brick with aluminum windows. It looked like what it was, a modern, well-designed and highly functional light manufacturing plant. There were three or four trees in front that gave partial shade to the small parking and entrance area, but the rest of the forty or fifty acres was bare, grass but no trees. The employee parking lot behind the building held three or four hundred cars and places for almost as many more. There was a chain link fence around the whole thing.

What McPhee thought was a rather small sign for the size of the operation spelled out Contel in aluminum letters set in a low brick wall.

A uniformed guard met him just inside the door. McPhee told him he wanted to speak to Mr. Bradham and that he was the sheriff. The guard spoke into a phone and then waved him to a pleasant-looking blonde behind an information desk. She gave him a friendly smile and told him Mr. Bradham's secretary would be here for him in just a moment.

McPhee glanced around the carpeted lobby and saw himself in a television monitor with the receptionist in the background. He unconsciously tightened his stomach muscles a little and ran his hand over the back of his head.

A trim, middle-aged, efficient-looking woman came down the wide hall.

"Sheriff McPhee? Mr. Bradham's office is this way, please. I'm Charlotte Coffin, Mr. Bradham's secretary." She smiled. "My oldest daughter went through high school with you. She was Sarah Butler then. Both she and I married since. What I mean is, she married and I remarried."

McPhee well remembered the dark-haired, bouncy cheerleader.

He smiled. "Sarah was too pretty to forget."

"Still is."

She ushered McPhee through the outer office, knocked, and opened the door to the inner office almost at the same time. Then she stood aside for him.

Bradham came round the desk, shook his hand, and said, "Sheriff McPhee," and motioned him to a seat.

He returned to his own high-back chair.

"Good to see you."

McPhee looked around the office admiringly. It was a large room, wainscoted in what looked to be walnut, with a matching desk and conference table. The pictures were mountains and streams, laurel and rhododendrons in bloom, and all the frames were in a light wood, probably birch.

"I like your office."

Bradham followed his eyes around the office.

"My wife decorated it for me, and Contel picked up

the tab, so really I can't take any credit. They told me it came to something like twenty-two thousand dollars."

McPhee appreciated the beauty of the office and tried to look impressed by the price tag.

"I wanted to talk to a few people about Mr. Jaynes's death on the river. We all know it was an accident, but I like to be thorough. I'm new on the job, as you probably know."

Bradham gave him a reassuring smile.

"I know, I voted for you."

"Well, thank you. I need all the help I can get."

"I appreciate what you're saying, Sheriff."

He was leaning forward, elbows on his desk, coat hung on a clothes tree in the corner.

"I just came from talking to Mrs. Jaynes."

He thought he'd better leave Lochmiller and his heavy-handed humor and logic out of it.

Bradham shook his head. "How's she taking it?"

McPhee cleared his throat.

"She seems to be all right. Taking it pretty well, I'd say."

Bradham leaned back in the chair.

"She's an unusual woman. Strong. One of the new breed."

They both nodded in silent understanding.

"As I say, Mr. Bradham, I need all the help I can get. I'm about to close the case and call it an accident. Do you know of any reason why I shouldn't?"

It came out well, and McPhee was pleased with himself.

Bradham leaned all the way back in his chair as if giving it considerable thought.

"No. No, I don't. I wondered a little how it could happen to a fellow like Jay Jay. He was really good, but then you never know."

His eyes came up briefly to meet McPhee's.

"Does the helmet business bother you?" McPhee asked. He watched for any trace of concern.

"The helmet? You mean the fact that he wasn't wearing one?"

"Well, I guess the fact that they couldn't find it. And then it suddenly appeared in the other truck."

"I don't have any problem with that, Sheriff. Both trucks were pretty much alike."

"Do you know when Mrs. Jaynes found it?"

"Not really. Perhaps after you left on Sunday. I remember she told me about it yesterday."

"Were you over there when Mr. Lochmiller came back, after he took Jaynes to the river?"

Bradham gave him a quick look. Then he shook his head and smiled again.

"No. I play golf Sunday mornings. I actually do just about live on the course. I love the game. You play?"

McPhee shook his head.

"Can't find the time."

"Well, I used to be that way. But now I've got my schedule so I can play two or three mornings a week. That's where I was Sunday morning, if you're asking. I tee off with the dawn, come back to have a good breakfast, and I'm ready for the day."

"Will everybody miss Jaynes, Mr. Bradham? Do you know of anyone who will be glad he's gone?"

"What kind of a question is that, Sheriff?"

"Just a simple one. Do you know of anyone who might have killed him?"

Bradham didn't pause. He treated it like a good company man would.

"Jay Jay Jaynes was a big man, Sheriff. He had American Operations right in the palm of his hand. Contel has fourteen plants in the United States plus this community development, and Jay Jay made it go."

It was as if McPhee had dared to put a stain on the godhead. He had his reaction. Bradham swiveled his chair to one side and looked out the window.

"We handle over twenty million dollars of defense contracts in this area alone. And we also have our Research and Development Division right here in the adjacent building. This was all Jay Jay's doing."

"So actually nobody stood to benefit?"

McPhee thought of Lochmiller and waited.

Bradham swung slowly back.

"You know what happened to the market when they got the news of Jay Jay's death?"

McPhee shook hs head, but he remembered.

"Twelve points off the first day."

McPhee nodded. Condolences were in order.

"What about his personal life?"

"He had no personal life."

It came out fast, and McPhee was sure Bradham was sorry he said it. Bradham looked down at the brown blotter on his desk. It went with the wood.

"He was truly a dedicated man." He said it slowly, with feeling.

McPhee didn't know what to say, so he said, "I'm sure he was."

"The sooner we're done with this whole thing, McPhee, the better off we'll all be. Believe me. It's my understanding that Contel is off again about six points today so far. If your department needs any additional help in confirming this accident, Sheriff, I'll be glad to call the governor."

McPhee was proud of himself. He was cool.

"Good of you to think of it, Mr. Bradham, but we should be done in a few days."

This was the second time somebody mentioned the governor. Maybe he had Contel stock as well. McPhee couldn't quite figure it out. Everyone was worried about the stock. Probably they all had a pretty good stake in it. Who knows? He'd got what he came for.

As he stood up to leave, there was a sharp rapping on the door. He looked at Bradham and then at the door. Bradham got up from his desk.

At that moment the secretary, Mrs. Coffin, came in.

"I just couldn't stop him, Mr. Bradham. I'm sorry."

"Who is it?"

"It's Lester."

"Tell him I'll be right with him."

When McPhee got to the outer office, Mrs. Coffin was standing next to her desk, on guard as it were. On the other side of the desk was a young man in his late twenties, slender, wearing glasses, and trembling all over. Mrs. Coffin nodded to him, and he went in and closed the door behind him.

Mrs. Coffin shook her head and started to walk McPhee down the hall.

"I just don't know what's happened to Lester. He's so on edge, every little thing."

"Who is he?"

"He's our chief supervisor in R and D. He's brilliant, but so edgy lately. He was going to bust right in on you."

"How long has he been this way?"

"Uh—it started last week."

McPhee expressed idle curiosity.

"What did you say his name was?"

"Lester Rennbarger. They hired him from California."

McPhee filed it and asked about Sarah.

"She's making me a grandmother again next month. How many do you have now, Sheriff?"

He thought of his wife in Raleigh and his dog at home.

"None. None so far, Mrs. Coffin."

He walked out the front door and wondered if he was becoming like Jay Jay, too dedicated to the wrong things.

11

Spur

McPhee turned the ignition key and it didn't catch. Even the car was slow to start. He pumped the gas and it finally came alive. It was Wednesday morning, and he wasn't sure how many hours he'd slept. He'd lain awake in the dark, looking at all the parts, and no matter how he tried, he couldn't get them to fit. Like some poorly rebuilt engine, there were always a few pieces lying around that didn't go anywhere. He'd had his run with the dog, and the dog was full of juice, and a little had rubbed off on him, but not much this morning.

As he came over the first rise he saw a small pickup coming down from Farney's place. Farney had a few acres back of McPhee's, just over the hill. He drove a road grader for the county, but he was usually gone from home by now. Went in real early. That wasn't his truck, either. Farney drove a big pickup. He watched it, about a half mile away, as it slowly came along a fence line. If it kept coming, it would come out on the road ahead of him. It disappeared behind some trees. He watched to see it emerge, but it never did. Must have stopped or slowed down.

McPhee tightened his grip on the wheel and pressed his foot down on the accelerator. Then he took a deep breath and let it out slowly. He eased off the gas. Every little thing was starting to get to him. He was letting his imagination get the better of him. He was seeing C.I.A., Russian agents, and hired gunmen behind every bush. He looked again and the truck had once more come into sight and was slowly coming down towards the road. McPhee would get to the fork first. Whoever it was would come out behind him. Could be some real estate agent casing Farney's six acres. Could be a hundred and one things. Let's settle back, McPhee, let's settle back and look at the hills. He opened the window and turned onto the highway. A little breakfast would help, too.

Courtney was seated at his table at the back, linen napkin, gray suit today. He greeted McPhee and went back to his granola, spooning it out studiously and methodically up over his chin. McPhee sat down and ordered two eggs over easy. He wasn't hungry, but a man had to eat.

Courtney dabbed at his mustache with the napkin.

"How's the dog?"

Courtney had given him the Brittany when he first came back, so he had a personal interest.

"Fine. Just fine."

"That's good." Courtney sipped a little coffee and went back to the granola.

"Sleep good?"

McPhee gave him a quick look.

"Does it show?"

"No. You look fine. Just making conversation. Haven't seen Foss for a couple of days. You seen him around?"

"Been busy."

"That fella in the river?"

McPhee nodded. The waitress brought his eggs.

"It's complicated. I'm seein' some folks this morning."

Courtney took this news in stride. He tilted the bowl to get the last of the granola.

A young fellow came in and sat down up front, sharp-looking suit, tie, and white shirt. McPhee studied him and wondered if he was carrying a gun. He looked for the telltale bulge. Turning his head back, Courtney caught his eye.

"He's a salesman, McPhee, sells auto parts."

"Mm." McPhee finished his eggs in silence.

As he got up to go, Courtney looked up at him.

"When you see Foss, tell him I was asking for him."

He didn't say if, he said when.

McPhee smiled. "I'll do that."

Courtney got around.

Mrs. Owens told him when he got back to the office that Lucas had called in and said he was waiting for McPhee over at the funeral home. He said he didn't get much sleep last night, but Spur was with him. Lucas might be a good ole boy, but when the chips were down, he delivered.

They were in the office of the Foss Funeral Home. Spurgeon senior was seated behind his desk, a modernistic chrome and glass affair with touches of black vinyl around the desk blotter and high-backed vinyl chair to match. The carpet was gray with thick sculpture, and the drapes were a heavy lavender material that effectively shut out almost all of the daylight. The lights, indirect around the ceiling, were all on, and McPhee was sitting next to the desk in what he presumed to be the bereaved-one's chair. Lucas sat next to him, and young Spur sat opposite. Spur made McPhee think of a young Greek god, except Greek gods didn't wear sweatshirts and tennis shoes and their hands didn't shake. They were long, thin hands, and he was massaging the fingers of one hand with the other. He knew they were shaking, and he was trying to hide it. Spur's mother had hands like that.

His eyes were confidently defiant, and there was a slight discoloration just below the left one. So far they had gotten nowhere.

"Spur, goddamn it, Spur, look at me."

Spur raised his eyes to his daddy's.

"Now these gentlemen represent the law. They are the law. I want you to answer their questions."

Spur looked back at him. At that point there was hate in his eyes.

Foss shook his head.

"I don't know. He could have this business. This whole thing could be his in a few years. Wants to go back to college, study psychology. He left once, now he wants to go back and fart around for another two years. I even said I'd do it if he'd come back here and grab hold for two full years, two full years is all I want, a fair trial period. But you know what he told me I could do with the funeral home?"

He looked at Lucas and then at McPhee. Both of them dropped their eyes. It wasn't hard to guess. They'd had run-ins with Spur before, and they knew Foss.

McPhee broke the silence. "I wonder, Foss, could I talk to Spur alone? You don't have to leave, and you can get a lawyer if you like. And Spur, you don't have to stay if you don't want to. You hear me?"

Spur looked up at him with a slight smile on his face.

"You giving me that Supreme Court crap?"

Foss interrupted. "It's for your own protection, Spur, can't you understand?" He opened his hands in a gesture of helplessness, got up, and walked out.

Lucas followed, closing the door quietly.

McPhee got out his notebook and began to read. Spur watched him warily out of the corner of his eyes. McPhee turned the page and continued reading. Spur sat up a little and looked around. McPhee could tell he was thinking of leaving.

"If you go anywhere, Spur, it will be straight to jail."

"Horseshit."

"Try me."

Spur looked at the door and then back at McPhee. "He drives me up the wall."

He ran his hand through his hair, bent forward, and put his elbows on his knees. "I don't know a goddamn thing about this whole business."

McPhee closed the notebook and looked over at him.

"I signed the ticket, put it in the box, and decided not to go. It was too cold and I didn't feel good, so I just drove around awhile. Then I went over to Hardee's and got a big beef with some fries and a shake. They saw me there, too."

McPhee looked at him, caught his eyes, and held them.

"You didn't tell me anything yet. Now, according to Gloria Jaynes. . . ." McPhee began looking through the notebook again trying to find the page.

"She wouldn't tell you anything."

"Why not? What's to hide? You do know her?"

"Sure, I know her. Great lady."

"See her often?"

"Once in a while. Other people know it, even the old man." He gestured towards the door.

"When did you see her last?"

"I don't remember, couple of days ago, maybe more."

"How well do you know her?"

"We were good friends."

McPhee pursed his lips and said, "Mmm," loud enough to be heard.

"What'd you say?"

"Nothing. Where did you see her?"

"Sometimes we went for a ride, sometimes over at her house. We were good friends."

"I know you were."

"What's that?"

"I said that I know you were good friends. Did you ever talk about her husband?"

"We talked about everything. That's the kind of lady she was, smart too. She understood about me and this," indicating the entire place around him, "dipshit, dog-robbin' operation. I hate the goddamn place."

McPhee, who shared some of his feelings about funeral homes, waited for a bit. Then he repeated his question.

"Did she ever talk about her husband?"

"Sure. He was something else."

"What do you mean 'something else'?"

"Run the world, screw the world, have a good time, and if you got in his way. . . . He didn't care about me and Gloria. Some people can be weird."

"Did you ever go jogging together?"

"Sure, we went jogging."

"What did Foss say about all this?"

"He said he'd kill me if he ever caught me with her again. And he meant it. He can go crazy, real crazy." He fingered the bruise on his cheek.

McPhee waited for a while. He had a pretty good idea where Spur had spent his time instead of being on the river.

"Did you really like her, Spur?"

The young fellow had covered his face with both hands and was wiping them slowly down his face.

"Spur, did you really like her?"

Spur shook his head, and McPhee thought he had wiped tears away. Spur shook his head again.

"I'm just not talking anymore. I'm done. Do anything you want. You goddamn people make me want to puke!"

McPhee closed the notebook, put it in his pocket.

"Maybe it's not so bad, Spur. We'll see."

And he got up and walked out.

Foss and Lucas were waiting outside. Foss was subdued and Lucas was worried. These were his friends.

McPhee took Foss to one side. "Did you tell Spur you'd kill him if he saw her again?"

Foss swung his head back and forth like a worried elephant.

"Well, you know how you will say something sometime? I was at the end of my rope. Stuff like this could ruin me in this town. I said it, but I didn't mean it. How else you gonna get through to the boy? Did he tell you anything?"

"Yeah, I think so. Nothin' much. Just that he had been seeing her and he liked her."

"You talk to her?"

McPhee nodded. "The kid's pretty torn up."

"You'll let me know?"

McPhee nodded again. "Sure, I'll keep in touch. Ah, Courtney was askin' for you. Said he missed you at breakfast."

Foss said, "Yeah, Courtney."

Foss put a hand on his arm.

"McPhee." Their eyes met. "Should I get a lawyer?"

McPhee looked away out the front door.

"No, not yet."

Lucas joined him and they started out.

Foss said, "Thanks, Sheriff."

It was the first time Foss had ever called him "sheriff." It had always been "McPhee."

12

The Banker

LUCAS AND MCPHEE stood at the foot of the steps to the funeral home. A florist's truck had just pulled up, and two cars were waiting to get into the parking lot. The traffic was stalled behind them. The clock on the courthouse said nine-thirty.

"What time's the funeral?"

Lucas said, "Two-thirty. My wife told me. They're letting some of them at the plant out early."

McPhee looked down at the curb.

"Where did you find him?"

"He was at a Buddy's Place over near Linville."

"Did he come along okay?"

"Sure, he didn't give me no trouble. I figured you were serious."

"Spur admitted he was going with her. He knows more than he's telling, but he's not ready to say much, yet."

Lucas studied the same part of the curb.

"I dunno, I just can't see the kid doin' it. But the kid with a woman like you say, who knows?"

"She could have told Spur when Jaynes was going, and she could have hidden the helmet."

"I don't think he would do it just on her say-so."

"Maybe he did it because he hated Jaynes, himself. He came on pretty strong when I mentioned his name."

"He did?"

"He sure did. Pure hate. Spur's got a hot streak."

Lucas conceded that. "He's got a hot streak all right."

"Billy get away to Atlanta all right?"

"I guess so."

They headed slowly back toward the new county building.

At the office McPhee told Lucas about his visit at the plant, and about Gloria and Lochmiller.

"Did he really say he'd hire somebody to kill him?" Lucas looked a little grim.

"He said it. But I think he was just being the big man. He'd had a few."

"But he said it." Lucas was adamant.

"Yeah. That doesn't prove a thing."

Then McPhee told him about Bradham and Lester Rennbarger. Lester bothered him.

"You got anything on for tomorrow?"

Lucas shook his head. "I was going to check on that cruiser over at the shop. They've had the thing almost a week. Waitin' on parts."

"This Lester works in research over there. He's all strung out, and I think we should find out why. Lester Rennbarger is his name."

Lucas looked at him.

"You know anything about him?"

"He's from California."

"Ah." Lucas said it as if that explained everything.

McPhee asked, "You goin' to the funeral?"

"Well, I. . . ." Lucas wasn't too big on funerals, or hospitals, or even doctor's offices, as far as that went.

McPhee didn't let him finish. "Good. I'll point him out to you at the funeral, and you can take it from there. You can change at lunchtime and get your pickup. I'll see you about two-fifteen. We'll go over together, right?"

"Right."

Mrs. Watson came to the door as Lucas was leaving.

"I forgot to tell you, Sheriff, but Mr. McKusick called from the bank. He wants you to drop over as soon as you get a chance."

She showed him the note. It said "McKusick, nine A.M."

George McKusick, president, chief stockholder, and chairman of the board all wrapped up in one, was waiting for him in his office. He was a man who took pride in the fact that thus far two or three large chains chose not to open branches in his county, and he had every intention of keeping it that way.

He was a big, heavyset man, expensively dressed, cuff links and all, with a fatherly manner, soft-spoken but firm. He had a habit of nodding his head a little as he spoke, in an indulgent if not patronizing way, leading people to believe that he had considered all they were saying before they opened their mouths.

"Have a chair, McPhee."

McPhee sat down. He tried to rid himself of the feeling that he was back in school and had been called to the principal's office. He stretched his long legs out in front of him and visually relaxed. It helped.

"How's the new program coming along, training the deputies on their off-duty hours?"

"Well, now that we've got a little money to pay them for the extra time, it's coming along fine."

McKusick smiled and nodded his head. "All boils down to finance, sooner or later, right, Sheriff?"

McPhee smiled back. "Sure helps."

"That's what I wanted to talk to you about."

He leaned forward and rested his arms on the desk.

"I'm concerned, McPhee, real concerned."

McPhee waited.

"This accident on the river. We're not making too much of it, are we?"

"What do you mean by that?"

"Well, once again it all comes down to finances, sooner or later."

He nodded his head and waited for McPhee. McPhee just looked at him. McKusick put his elbows on the desk and lowered his voice.

"Do you have any idea at all, McPhee, what that payroll out at Contel amounts to every single week of the year?"

McPhee decided to let him play out his hand.

"Quite a bit, I'd say."

"Over two hundred thousand dollars. And do you know what Contel's taxes are between the Emerald Valley Community and the plant? It amounts to over thirty per cent of the entire tax revenue of the county; thirty per cent."

"I'm impressed."

"You should be, McPhee. Four or five hundred jobs for our people, our people, McPhee, the same people that elected you sheriff of this county. And thirty per cent of your own budget. This company means a lot to us, and I think we should listen when they have something to say."

"Just what did they have to say?"

"They asked me to talk to you, Sheriff. They appreciate all the help they received during the recent tragedy they had down there with Jaynes being drowned, and all. They wanted me to tell you just how thankful they are to every man in your department who helped out. They also appreciate your further investigations confirming the fact that it was an accident. And now that we're all agreed on that, they would also appreciate the matter being closed."

McPhee felt a little sick. He knew about politics and power structures when he took the job. But this could be murder. This was no speeding ticket or a drunken teenager. He felt the blood rising to his head, and he almost started to shoot back. Instead, he counted to ten, slowly.

McKusick cleared his throat.

"I can understand that, in a way."

"What do you mean, 'in a way'?"

"Well, I guess the stock dropped a little. The market is always sensitive to these things."

"And rightly so . . . Go ahead, McPhee, I didn't mean to interrupt."

McKusick's head was nodding now in hearty agreement.

"But we're not fully convinced that it was an accident."

The head stopped nodding, and McKusick leaned back in his chair.

McPhee continued. "The man was an expert with a canoe, he'd run the river many times."

"And those are the kind that get overconfident, right, especially in high water?"

He looked expectantly at McPhee, ready to nod again.

"Possibly. We also have doubts that the body could have floated by itself to where it was found, and we wonder where the helmet was."

He decided not to tell him about the bloodstain, and he couldn't mention the F.B.I. Maria had made that plain. He'd gone about as far as he could go. To hell with McKusick.

"Can't you clear all that up, McPhee? After all, the funeral's this afternoon, and we should bury the whole thing. Right?"

He started to nod but held his head, waiting for McPhee's reaction.

McPhee looked at his feet. The sick feeling had left, and he no longer felt he was in anybody's office but McKusick's. McKusick was off base and if he didn't know it, he had to be told.

"Wrong."

It came out softly but very clear.

"This could be murder, and we're not about to bury the whole thing."

He looked up at McKusick and then back down to his shoes. He felt better.

McKusick shook his head. He was not about to give up on this young fellow.

"I voted for you, McPhee. We have confidence in your judgment, but these are good people, McPhee. All they're trying to do is to protect the name of their company and get back to business as usual. And they're big people with defense contracts worth millions. They are important to the nation as well as this county, and it's our job to help them as much as we can."

It was starting to get to McPhee, but he kept his eyes on his shoes.

"McKusick," he purposely dropped the Mr., "you're good people too, important to the county. But if it happened to you instead of this Jaynes fellow, I'd do exactly the same thing. I wouldn't close the case until I was sure of what happened."

He raised his eyes to see how the banker was taking it.

He seemed to be thinking it over. Actually, he was considering that if it had happened to him, it probably would be better for the bank if the case were closed quickly. No mess. No fuss. But he didn't say so.

McPhee decided to let him down easily.

"It may be that we'll all know a little more in a few days. You never know in these cases."

McPhee spoke as if he'd handled cases like this before.

McKusick answered slowly. "Well, I suppose a few more days won't hurt too much. It's just not good for business."

He came around to the other side of the desk, and they shook hands.

"One question, McKusick?"

"Yes?"

"Who called you?"

"They've got a fellow out there in public relations. Said they all hoped it wouldn't go on too long. Just not good for business."

McPhee left. He didn't feel too bad. He wondered if an unsolved murder could really be good for business.

13

The Funeral

McPhee heard there were at least six corporate jets out at the airfield, and the Keebler House had been jammed for lunch. People in a line outside. So far, two out-of-town TV crews had shown up, plus the local one that had been mentioning the funeral all morning. Large numbers of local people were there, some to attend the funeral, others just to watch. Some heard that the governor was coming, and others said Senator Haines might come. There was also a rumor that Burt Reynolds and Sally Field might show up.

The *Chronicle* still played up the story, "Jaynes's Funeral Today," and they told of who might possibly be attending as well as the preparations made by the Foss Funeral Home.

Down in the right-hand corner they'd carried a smaller headline, "Sheriff Completing Investigation." McPhee was quoted as saying that he thought the investigation would be completed in a day or two and they had to run down one or two more leads before they could be certain there had been no possible foul play.

When asked if there had been any new evidence, the sheriff said, "Nothing of any consequence." The article went on to mention that Jaynes had been an expert with a canoe and there had been some question as to why he was not wearing a helmet. It also stated there had been "strangers on the river," whatever that meant. McPhee hadn't told them about Spur, and he hadn't mentioned the bloodstains. He had decided to keep those things quiet as long as he could.

McPhee had read that even the secretary of defense might be there. He mentioned this to Lucas as they walked across the square. He couldn't remember and he asked Lucas if he knew the name of the secretary of defense.

Lucas shook his head. "They change those fellas around, don't they?"

McPhee conceded the point.

Foss had opened all three of his chapels together and also opened each onto a terrace. It was a mild day, so it promised to work out well. There was to be no graveside service, and there had been no viewing. Just a memorial service today, with interment at a later date. Rumor had it that Jaynes was to be cremated.

McPhee and Lucas took up a spot in the middle chapel where they could, by moving a step or two, see almost all present. The closed coffin was at the end, with only four flower arrangements. Two rows were set aside for family and another two rows for corporate officials. Foss's men seemed to know who they all were.

Courtney came by in a dark blue suit, looked real dapper. He nodded to McPhee and Lucas.

"Good turnout. Nothing like a funeral to bring people together. Something we all have in common."

He slipped in a few rows towards the front and sat down.

By two-thirty the seats were pretty well filled, and a few people were standing, like McPhee and Lucas. Many were people from the plant.

McPhee spotted him about six rows from the front, bushy hair, long neck, and glasses. He nudged Lucas.

"There's your man, Lester Rennbarger, the R and D man from the plant." He counted, "Sixth row back, third from the center on the left."

Lucas picked him out and kept his eyes fixed on the man.

Lochmiller and Mrs. Jaynes came in then, and the Bradhams along with three strangers. McPhee pointed them out to Lucas as well, one at a time.

McPhee looked at the three heads in a row—Lochmiller, Bradham, Gloria. Somehow he thought that one of them might be congratulating himself—or herself—or perhaps they were joined together in an unholy trinity, but he felt the answer was there.

Lucas noted that Lester kept looking at the people up front, but he couldn't tell whether Lester was watching Bradham or Gloria Jaynes.

Olin Wheatly, the Presbyterian preacher, spoke of Mr. Jaynes's "remarkable career in the world of finance, and his leadership in the field of electronic communications." He also noted "his love of natural beauty, the hills, the trees, and the rivers."

One of which, thought McPhee, proved to be his downfall.

The minister mentioned "tragic accident" three times and "untimely accident" once.

McPhee wondered what a "timely accident" was like.

It was a fine service. Wheatly finished by reading two or three of the familiar psalms for the bereaved, and McPhee thought of Gloria and her "conveniences." If some of those present were holding their breaths for her to break down, they were going to be disappointed. The ladies would say she was being brave.

Then Foss came on stage and said that the service was over.

McPhee and Lucas stepped onto the terrace. No one seemed to be going anywhere.

McPhee said, "Where you parked?"

Lucas gestured over to the entrance of the parking lot. Two cars down from the entrance was Lucas's pickup. He could pull out any time.

McPhee had told him to follow Lester, put him to bed tonight, and get to his home by six in the morning and stay with him until he got to work. McPhee was playing a hunch.

"Got your gun?"

"In the truck."

McPhee looked at him.

"Now take care, Lucas. If somebody killed Jaynes, they could kill again. Take care."

He wanted to tell Lucas the whole story, F.B.I. and all, but he knew it would blow his mind. Besides, Maria had made it very plain that it was for him only to know.

"Be careful."

Lucas spotted his prey and took off.

People were still talking, and very few seemed ready to leave. McPhee couldn't tell whether Lochmiller drifted over to him by design or happenstance. The man spoke to him, smiling.

"You're still not too bright, eh, McPhee?"

McPhee just listened.

"I'm leaving tonight for Atlanta in our company jet, but I'll be back tomorrow, Thursday night, McPhee. Maybe you can arrange to close the case by then."

The man seemed to be deadly serious. McPhee looked around to see if anyone else was close enough to have heard, but they were very much alone.

"Hear me well, McPhee."

He turned and walked away.

McPhee thought he recognized a threat when he heard one. He wondered if he would hear from the governor, the secretary of defense, or possibly a stranger from Atlanta who was on Lochmiller's payroll.

14

Billy's Trip to Atlanta

BILLY SAT IN the front seat of the Dodge Horizon and Julie sat next to him. They had just had a good breakfast at the Country Inn, where 321 joined the interstate. Billy had eaten a stack with a double order of sausage, and Julie had eggs. Billy said the pancakes were good, but not as light as hers. She considered this and said, "They probably don't beat 'em as much."

It was raining, but they both felt as if they were a part of a romantic adventure. When Julie got herself duckied up, most people knew she was around. He'd seen two or three fellows turn around as he'd followed her out of the dining room.

When they got back in the car, Julie reminded him of that Chinese place where they had gone dancing just west of Atlanta when they had been there a couple of years ago. He remembered. It was a good time, things were looking up!

"They'll have a man drive me around town there, so you can have the car. Maybe shop a little. We probably should check into the motel first, don't you think?"

"What for?" Julie reached forward to adjust the radio.

"Well, you know, we can get unpacked and you can call your cousin and I can call Curtis."

Julie found Willie Nelson on the radio, adjusted the volume and sat back. They both listened to that reedy old voice . . . "for you're always on my mind, you are always on my mind."

"Did you know he was an old man before he started making a lot of money?"

"No," said Billy. He'd never thought about it very much.

The rain was coming down hard now. He thought of Jaynes and that big house and McPhee and his wife, and Spurgeon. He relaxed a little more and dropped his hands to rest on the bottom of the wheel. He wasn't doing so bad, all things considered. And the boy, he liked that coon tail.

When they got unpacked, Billy called Curtis and Curtis said he'd pick him up in about a half hour, right at the motel. Julie and he agreed to meet back at the motel around six-thirty. He said he'd call if he was going to be late. Julie kissed Billy, and he watched her take off in the Horizon.

He stood in the lobby now. Some folks were checking out, paying their bills. God, forty-five dollars for a place to sleep! McPhee wouldn't believe it.

Billy saw a Mustang pull into the drive with a big black man at the wheel. His head almost touched the roof. Billy went out and shook hands with McPhee's friend Curtis through the window and then went around and got in. Curtis drove through the heavy traffic and listened while Billy told the story. They finally came to a run-down apartment complex.

Curtis said, "340 Silverland Drive, here we are." They pulled up.

Billy asked, "How do you know he's home?"

Curtis said, "He's home. I called and asked for Mr. Zybarski. He said, 'Yes' and then I told him he'd won a prize but he'd have to come down to Brown's Furniture Store to collect it."

"What'd hc say?"

"He hung up. But he's there."

They went in the entryway. There were six doorbells and a little card above each. Zybarski was 2C. Curtis pushed the bell and nothing happened. He pushed it again. Still nothing.

Billy whispered, "Maybe he went to the furniture store."

Curtis just looked at him, and he stopped halfway up the stairs and turned to Billy.

"We don't know anything about this guy, right?"

"Right."

"You want to let me handle it? Maybe he killed the guy, right?"

"Right."

"Well, let me go ahead, then. This is my home turf."

Billy didn't argue.

They found 2C. It was the first door on the left. Curtis knocked and stepped back to the left of the door. He motioned Billy back towards the door to the other apartment.

"You cover for me."

He formed the words with his mouth without making a sound.

There was no answer, so Curtis knocked again.

Billy could see now that whoever opened the door would not see anyone at first. They'd probably open the door wider and step out a little.

They heard a scraping and steps inside the apartment. Billy's hand dropped to his gun. Some more steps and then the door opened a crack, held by a chain. He saw a barefoot man in shorts, and he recognized the bearded face, but the man didn't see him. The man inside unlatched the door and stuck his head out.

"Detective Curtis, Atlanta Police Department. Your name Zybarski?"

"Yeah."

"We want to talk to you."

Curtis pushed the door open and the man back inside, all in one motion. Billy followed him, his hand still resting on the butt of his gun.

"This the guy?"

Billy nodded. "Yeah, that's him."

"What's this about?"

There was a small alcove off the kitchen with a dining table and four chairs. Curtis motioned him over to the table.

"Now wait a minute!"

Curtis told him to sit down.

"I want to get dressed first. I just got out of bed."

"Sit down."

The man sat down and looked at Curtis, scared. He hitched the chair away from the table.

Curtis said, "Check the apartment."

Billy did, and when he came back he said, "It's okay, nobody."

Then Curtis sat down, pulled out his notebook and laid it on the table. The man looked at the notebook and then back at Curtis. Billy took a chair and moved it back from the table near the wall where he could see the guy's hands. Then he sat down.

He wasn't a big guy, but wiry, stringy muscles. No hair on his chest at all.

"You were on the river up in Bryson County last weekend, right?"

"Right."

"You know what happened up there?"

"You mean the guy that drowned? Yeah, we saw it on television, Steve and me. You talked to Steve?"

Curtis nodded. "Yeah, we talked to Steve. He didn't make a hell of a lot of sense, but we talked to him."

Billy noted the outright lie, but Curtis had said it well. Keep the guy off balance.

Billy passed a copy of his "put in" ticket to Curtis.

"You guys put in at about seven-thirty?"

The guy inched over to look at the copy and nodded his head. You could tell he was thinking, now, and getting his act together.

"See anybody else when you put in, any cars, pickups in the parking lot?"

The man shook his head slowly, looking at Curtis, wondering what he knew before he said too much.

"So what happened next?"

"We went down the river."

Billy looked at him.

"There was just you and Steve, and you left your car at the 'put in'?"

The man looked at Billy and started to nod his head. Billy picked it up.

"How were you going to get back to the truck, after you finished your run?"

But the guy was ready for him. He had it figured.

"We got a system, see. We take turns. I put in and go down to the shoals and Steve, he meets me there and then he goes down and I take the truck to the lake. Then we put the canoe in the truck and go home."

Curtis looked at Billy and Billy just looked at the table. He picked up an ashtray that was in the middle of the table and seemed to be examining it for flaws. Curtis had had time to think about it.

"So only you put in by yourself?"

He looked at the ticket.

"It says 'two' in the party, right here."

"Well, there was two. Only one at a time. That's a safety feature, and we figured we had it covered since the other guy would be waiting. Besides, that was the only way we could do it, with just one car."

Billy had to hand it to him. If he was lying, it sounded pretty good.

"So you went down the river by yourself from where you put in to the shoals, is that it?"

"Yeah, that's it."

Billy looked at him.

"When you talked to me on the river you said your buddy was on down the river."

"He was, he was waiting in the truck."

There was a pause.

"So what did you see?"

"If you talked to Steve, I guess he told you."

He looked at Billy and then at Curtis.

Billy couldn't tell. He looked for some sign with the guy that might give him away, but the guy had it together now, and he came out with the story slowly and deliberately.

"Well, first I hit the narrows, you know where the rock on each side of the river comes almost together. There's actually waves there, the current is that strong. Waves maybe two feet high."

Billy nodded, but Curtis just listened, looking at the notebook. "It sets you up pretty good. Gets your attention, you know?" He looked around a little to see if he was coming across well. Billy looked at the ashtray, and Curtis kept his eyes on the notebook.

"After that, I took the Big Bend, you know. There's a drop, and you have to put it right in there. It's rated a Number IV."

Curtis looked up. "Never mind the travelogue. What did you see?"

"Well, as I told Steve, I was just coming up on Bull Sluice, and it was starting to get a little lighter."

"What time was it when you hit the sluice?"

"Maybe a little after eight-thirty. There was still some fog, and I pulled up just this side of the sluice and went to take a look."

Both sets of eyes were on him now, and he knew it.

"I saw somebody walk into the water and push an empty canoe into the current."

Billy stared at him. "Why didn't you tell me about it when I talked to you on the river?"

"I didn't want to get involved."

Curtis looked at him in complete disbelief. "You see a guy get killed on the river and you don't want to get involved? What kind of smoke is that?"

"I didn't see anybody get killed. All I saw was somebody walk into the water and push an empty canoe into the current."

The guy had it down pat, almost too pat. He said it like a stuck record, and then he looked down at his hands. Billy and Curtis stared at him.

"That's all I saw."

"So what happened? Did he stand there and wave as you went by?"

Billy asked, "Was it a man or a woman?"

"I couldn't tell, had a hat on, big straw hat."

"What else?"

Zybarski shook his head. "That's all. I was near a bush, and I just squatted down and waited. Pretty soon I heard an engine start up, and when I looked again, I couldn't even see the canoe, nothin'."

Curtis looked disgusted. "You see the body?"

Zybarski looked at him and shook his head.

Curtis said, "Get your clothes on."

Zybarski got up and went into the bedroom. Curtis followed him and stood at the door.

Billy looked out the window and saw the tall downtown buildings in the distance. Jesus, there were a lot of people in Atlanta.

They got the statement from Zybarski downtown at his office. Exactly like he told it at the apartment.

And they also got the statement from Steve, word for word, "I didn't see it but he told me. Somebody walked into the water and pushed an empty canoe into the current." Same line.

Later they were standing next to Curtis's car out in the parking lot. Curtis was explaining. "I talked to the captain. He said there just wasn't enough to hold them. They both got a few things on the record, but as I told you before, it's not much. They're not going anywhere."

Billy looked at the cars, people on the street, the buildings set almost one on top of another, no trees. It was different. An ambulance came wailing down the street. Nobody seemed to notice.

"What time you leavin', Billy?"

"After we get up tomorrow. Julie and me, well, we thought we'd have a night on the town."

Curtis's face broke into a wide grin. "Why not? Come on, I'll take you home."

On the way back to the motel, Curtis looked at him sideways. "It's different down here, right?"

"Yeah, sure is. You know how many bank robberies we had last year?"

Billy really didn't want to know. "How many?"

"Seventy-four. Banks, not shop and go's or liquor stores, banks. It's a jungle." Curtis seemed almost proud of the fact.

"That's a lot."

Billy tried to think back to when somebody robbed a bank in Bryson County. He couldn't remember. He looked at Curtis. "Is it getting better or worse?"

"Who knows? Maybe a little better, but who knows?"

"It's where the action is, right?"

"Oh, yeah, plenty, all kinds. It's not so bad. We got the Braves and the Falcons. And we have a lot of plays, concerts, stuff like that. Lot goin' on in Atlanta."

Billy nodded as Curtis swung into the center lane, hesitated a moment with a foot on the brake, and then with a burst of speed swung between the oncoming cars and pulled into the motel.

"I'll see they drop off those statements first thing in the morning."

They shook hands then, and Billy thanked him. Offered to buy him a drink.

Curtis sat there in the car and shook his head. "Thanks, anyway, but I got to get home. My wife works too, and the kids will be waiting for me."

"Sure, sure." It took him a little time to digest what Curtis said—action, robberies, Braves, Falcons, concerts, and the kids home alone. He waved him out of the driveway and headed into the lobby to call McPhee. It wouldn't go through the switchboard if he called from the phone in the lobby. Billy called collect. It was about five-thirty.

"I'm calling from the motel. Everything okay back home?"

"Fine, Billy, just fine. How did you make out?"

"Well, that's why I called. Curtis was very nice to me down here. Took me out to see both those guys."

"Same ones you saw on the river?"

"Well, I only saw one, remember, but he was the same one. His buddy was waiting downriver with the truck. They took turns. I saw the one just below the sluice."

"Yes, I remember now."

"Well, you know it's funny what he told me. He said he came down to a place just above the sluice. He wanted to look it over before he went through, high water, you know?"

McPhee didn't say anything.

"You there? You hear me, Pete?" Billy talked loud.

"Ycah, I'm here."

"He said he saw somebody walk into the water and push an empty canoe into the current."

"Could he identify him?"

"Nope."

"Was it a man, a woman, a boy, or what?"

"He couldn't tell."

"You called it, eh, Billy?"

"Yeah. It sounded like what we both thought, remember? I figured this was important and I better call."

"I'm glad you did. Did your fellow see the body?"

"No. He said he didn't. And he said he didn't tell me before because he didn't want to get involved. This is pretty big stuff, right, Pete?"

"Yeah. Probably as close to an eyewitness as we'll ever get. You get the statements?"

"Yeah. Curtis is getting them typed up. They've got stenographers down here, McPhee. You know?"

"I heard. Stenographers."

"He said he'd get the statements signed and bring them by in the morning."

"Billy."

"Yeah."

"You think these fellas were on the level? You believe them?"

"Who knows. People lie pretty good these days but . . . yeah, I guess so." There was a silence on the line.

"Billy?"

"Yeah."

"You know Lochmiller?"

"Sure, the fellow with the big head."

"He's flying into Atlanta tonight on Contel's company jet. Do you think you could get Curtis to put a man on him when he gets in?"

"Yeah, but how will he know him?" Billy saw his night on the town slowly disappearing into the sunset.

"No, never mind. I can take care of it from here. Forget it."

Billy was resigned. "I can take care of it if you need me, Pete. I could go with him."

"No, thanks anyway, but I can handle it from up here."

"Sure?"

"Yes, it's okay. And this is great, Billy. You hit the bull's-eye."

"Thanks, Pete. Julie and me, well, we're going out tonight. I promised her."

"Have a good time. See you back here at about what, ten-thirty?"

"I'll be there, Pete, with those statements."

When Billy hung up he climbed the stairs to the second floor where their room was. He noted the little green Horizon parked down at the end of the lot. Julie'd be there.

She was lying on the bed when he came in, her hair all wrapped up in a towel, a newspaper in her hand. He kissed her, took off his jacket, and flopped down in the chair.

"It's advertised. That Chinese place, so it's still open. They got the same band, too."

Billy began taking off one of his shoes. "You know, Julie, it's different down here." He wondered if Zybarski bashed the guy, or maybe his buddy. He could have had the bucket in the truck.

"I know. We don't have any place that serves Chinese food. But you know that empty place down on Main Street towards the bridge?"

Billy didn't but he said, "Yeah?"

"I heard they were going to start one up down there real soon."

Billy took off the other shoe. "Mm."

"I already took my shower, so you go ahead."

After the egg rolls and the sweet and sour pork, they talked about their boy Johnny, and about the trails and the wild flowers and the waterfalls, and drank some more wine. Then they danced.

That night they lay side by side in the motel, their

bodies touching. And the places where they touched were a little warmer. He put his arm around her, and she snuggled into him.

They could hear the traffic outside. It was almost so noisy you couldn't hear anything. A truck shifted five times as it pulled out into the traffic, and a siren sounded in the distance. He heard some people coming along the passageway outside. They'd had a few. He was saying, "Honey, when we hit that sack," and as they passed by, she said "Ah, you devil, you!" They lay there listening to the city noises in the darkness.

"It's different down here. Sure is."

"But we're not."

"That's right, Julie." Then she turned to him, and the city noises faded away.

15

McPhee's Notes and the Night Visitor

McPHEE HUNG UP after talking with Billy. He got up and closed the door to his office. Nobody was out there except the dispatcher in his cubbyhole. McPhee wanted to be sure he wasn't overheard. He looked in his wallet and found Maria's card.

He dialed the number. She said he could reach her at any time at that number. He listened to it ring on the other end of the line. A male voice answered, "This is 841-1785, who is it you're calling, please?"

"Orsini, Maria Orsini."

"One moment, please."

"Yes." He recognized her voice.

"This is McPhee."

"Right, McPhee. How are things up in the mountains?"

"Well, they're moving along. That's why I called." Then he told her about Lochmiller at the funeral and what he thought was a threat. When he was done, he asked if he could get surveillance on him. "He's coming into Atlanta this evening on Contel's company jet."

"Yeah. We can handle that. No problem. I just don't understand. What do you think he's up to?"

"I have no idea." He told her about his other conversation. About Lochmiller saying he could hire a killer here in the States for about five thousand.

There was a silence on the other end. "Maria?"

"Well, he's got the price about right. That's all I can say."

"Is this a clear line?"

"Well, it's probably being taped, but no one will hear that's not supposed to. We have people working for us who don't know we're with the F.B.I. That's why we run our calls through this special operator."

"I'm reasonably certain Jaynes was murdered."

"Mm."

"You hear me?"

"Sure. You're not about to make an arrest, nothing like that, McPhee?"

"No, but. . . ." He looked out and saw someone in the outer office talking with the dispatcher.

"When you coming up?"

"I'll make it tomorrow. Dinner for sure. But I'll call you, okay?"

The "okay" had a tender quality to it, not at all like an F.B.I. agent. It sounded like a woman, a real woman. "Good, you'll give me a ring?"

"Yes. I will, McPhee. Bye."

"Bye."

McPhee put the phone down. He tried to sort out his thoughts. Here he was with a murder on his hands, and the thing that shook him most was that "okay" with the soft overtone. He tried to think about Lochmiller and his getting lost. Then Gloria and Spur, and Bradham and Lester. But the only question he seemed to be able to focus on was whether or not Maria would get a motel room before she came out to his place.

It was getting dark when he left the office. He went across the street over to Miller's Market and got a sirloin, plus a couple of marrowbones for the dog.

When he drove up to his house, the dog was waiting on the porch, just sitting there. McPhee gave him one of the bones, went in, took off his clothes, and took a long, hot shower. He was bushed and uptight. The shower eased him down.

He put on shorts and a sweatshirt, got a beer out of the refrigerator, and then made supper—broccoli, a salad, and the steak in the broiler for eight minutes. He set the timer.

Taking a long yellow pad out of the drawer, along with two ball point pens, he set them on the table and sat looking at them until the timer went off.

He ate supper, got another beer, and let the dog in. The dog wanted the scraps, so he fed Brook and came back to look at the yellow pad.

At the top of the page he wrote "Lochmiller." He left a few lines and wrote "Gloria," then "Bradham," and "Spur." Then he added "Lester" and put a question mark after it. he tore that page off and set it to one side. Starting at the top again, he wrote these sentences:

"The murderer must have known when Jaynes was going down the river."

"The murderer must have known the location of Bull Sluice."

"The murderer must have removed the helmet from the truck."

"The murderer cannot account for where he/she was at that time." He skipped a couple of lines and wrote some more:

"Why was he killed?"

"Was there an accomplice?"

One by one he walked each of them through the possibilities: Lochmiller, Gloria, Bradham, Spur, and Lester. The helmet bothered him with the last two, but Gloria could have helped out there. She would have had no trouble with the helmet. He tried to picture Gloria with that grapefruit-sized rock in her hand and that faraway look in her eyes, bringing it down on the back of his head and saying to herself, "You are no longer a convenience to me!"

He'd filled up almost half the pad, and three empty beer cans sat on the table. Maybe there'd be a break. Lucas or Billy might have a few answers, or even Maria. But it was there for sure, and it was his. He'd give it his best shot.

He went to bed.

McPhee didn't know if he'd been to sleep or not. He rolled over and looked at the clock. The digits said 3:45. The room was dark except for the dim glow from the clock. No light from the window. It was black outside. No moon. He sat up, swung his legs off the bed, and went into the bathroom. He got a glass of water, and as he was setting the glass back in the holder, he stopped, his hand in midair.

Moving his head slowly, he raised his eyes to the window. Was that a flicker of light? He moved to the window. Pitch black outside. Then he saw it again. Just a faint glow over by the shed. He watched for a moment to be sure. Silently, he went back to the bed, slipped on shorts and slippers, and lifted his revolver off the nightstand. The dog whimpered, and McPhee held his breath. The last thing he wanted was for that dog to start barking. He scratched the dog's head and whispered that it was all right. The dog quieted down.

The flashlight was on top of the dresser. He padded quietly to the phone.

"This is McPhee. I'm at home. There's a prowler out

back and I want a car on the valley road to my place as soon as possible. No lights or siren. Got it?" He hung up.

Then he went out the front door and eased along to the corner of the house, the flashlight in one hand, the .38 in the other. It was black out by the shed. Then the small glow came on again. The prowler was at the canoe. When McPhee was halfway there, the light went out. McPhee leveled the gun and holding the light out to one side, he flicked it on.

"Hold it, or I'll shoot!"

For an instant the man was frozen in the light, then he bolted.

McPhee let him have one, low, and heard a sharp cry of pain. He tried to find him again with the light, but the figure had disappeared around the corner of the house. McPhee went after him. He pointed the light out towards the road. The front yard was empty. The dog was barking up a storm in the house. McPhee kept covering the yard with the light, eased over to the front door, and let the dog out. The dog made for the shed and then came tracking around the corner of the house. He waited for the dog to see if it would take off on the man's tracks, but no such luck.

He went out to the road, throwing the beam of light at the trees and bushes, but there was no sign. He trekked back to the house, called in the dog, turned on the light, and slipped out to the back door. Back at the road he stood waiting, listening. At one time, he thought he heard movements down the road, so he started down, slowly and quietly, stopping to listen in the blackness of the night.

Far down the road he heard it. The noise of a cycle starting, then gradually fading out. It stopped. McPhee waited. There were lights down the road, now. Then they were coming up towards him, and he crossed the road to be on the driver's side.

It was Cecil Nellis, a six months' recruit, and Cecil was playing it cool. "Heard him coming, Sheriff, and caught him in the dark, square in the middle of the front bumper."

"Is he hurt?"

"He got scratched up a little when he went flying off the bike. Maybe something wrong with one leg. I told him I'd blow his head off if he tried anything. Figured I'd better let him know his rights."

McPhee could see he was pleased with himself. "You did all right, Cecil. Did he have a gun?"

"Yep. This little number." He held up what looked to be a .32 automatic.

"You talk to him?"

"He won't talk, Sheriff, so I just locked him up in the back and came on up here."

McPhee got in the other side of the cruiser, and they went back to the house.

"You want to get him out?"

"No. Just let me have a look."

He turned the flashlight on the man in the back seat and looked at him through the grille. "You all right?"

"Yeah. That guy came right at me with his lights out."

It was not an accusation, simply a statement of fact with a touch of respect. Evidently Nellis wanted to be certain he made contact.

"Who are you and what were you after?" He shifted the light from his face onto the man's chest.

The man just shook his head, "I don't have anything to say, nothing."

He'd never seen the man before, clean shaven, black nylon jacket, about twenty-five or thirty, not country, and probably not local, by the sound of him.

"You shot me, too." This, also, was not said with any malice. Just a fact. McPhee was pleased on two counts. He hadn't missed and it wasn't a critical wound.

Prowlers could be anybody, including a neighbor or a neighbor's kid.

"Where you hit?"

The man put one leg forward, and McPhee could see a bloody calf.

He turned to Nellis. "Call in and tell them you got the prowler and that you're bringing him in. Have them give the emergency room at the hospital a ring, too. We'll stop there first. I'll get some clothes on and follow right behind you. What did you do with the cycle?"

"After I got him locked in the back, I pushed it into the bushes. Got the tag number. What do you suppose he was after, Sheriff?"

McPhee lied slowly and convincingly. "I don't know, Nellis. I just don't know."

It was almost six o'clock when they got back to the office. They had stopped off at the emergency room and had the scratches and bullet wound treated. It had gone through the fleshy part of the man's calf just missing the bone.

He had no identification and still refused to give any information at all, even after having his rights read to him. McPhee worked on him for twenty minutes, but the man wouldn't say a word.

McPhee told Nellis to book him and lock him up and check on the cycle tag. Then he looked at himself in the mirror—beard, dark circles, bloodshot eyes, weary all the way.

"Let him make a call if he wants, when you can get around to it. I'm going home for a shave and shower. I'll be back in an hour or two."

He was about to commend Nellis again and thought better of it. Might go to his head. He was still pretty young.

16

Lucas in the Pines

MARTHA, HIS WIFE, didn't like the idea at all. Lucas had come home at eleven that evening and slipped into the big double bed as quietly as possible. Just as he was about to go to sleep, she got up and went to the bathroom. He watched her out of his half-shut eyes. She was a big-boned woman, no fat. She hadn't necessarily taken care of her figure, she had just worked all her life, and borne and raised their three sons. She got back into bed.

"Where you been?"

"Like I said, followin' that fellow."

"What'd he do?"

"We don't know. That's why I'm followin' him."

Martha frumped around in the bed and rolled over. "You think he killed that Jaynes fellow?"

Lucas rolled over on his side, away from her, one arm beneath his head, the way he always slept. "Maybe."

Martha said, "Humph. You take care of yourself, Lucas."

When she got no answer, she said, "You hear?"

"I heard, Martha, I heard."

She rolled away from him then. This was the way they always slept, backsides just touching. Lucas liked her just being there. Then he went to sleep.

It was dark when he slipped out of the house next morning. No moon, no first light, just dark. He set the thermos next to him on the seat and drove down towards town. The kid lived over on the other side in a duplex on the edge of town. He'd followed him there last night. He shut off the lights on the pickup and backed into a little grove of trees about half a block away and rolled down the window. A dog barked over on the other side of a pasture. Lucas bent down and put the flashlight on his watch: quarter to six. That should be early enough. He poured a little coffee out of the thermos and settled down to wait.

Maybe twenty minutes later a light came on in the duplex. Lucas shifted. His .38 was stuck a little under his thigh. He freed it up. The day's light was coming now, just a little grayness before the dawn. Pretty soon the kid came out of the duplex, got in the Volkswagen, and drove off towards town. Lucas followed but kept his lights off.

The kid went through town and took the highway out towards Emerald Valley. Lucas perked up. Maybe McPhee's hunch would pay off. McPhee wasn't too bad anyway, nice enough, young, but smart. Martha had heard from the secretary down at the bank that he'd told McKusick where to head in. He didn't look it, but he was gutsy, too. It was a little easier in the department since he took over. People talked a little more to each other. The sun was starting to show now, and he kept his eyes on the taillights of the Volkswagen up ahead.

About a mile past the entrance to Emerald Valley, the Volkswagen slowed down and turned off to the right into the woods. Lucas slowed and went on past. It was just a trail, two tracks overgrown. He pulled up, parked well off the road, and listened. He could hear the Volkswagen's motor not too far away, just idling along. Lucas backed the truck into the brush and got out. He could see now. The sun was just starting over the ridge. He got out, closed the door quietly, arranged his holster on his side, and felt for his pocketknife in his pants. He never liked goin' into the woods without a knife. Then he started down the trail. He couldn't hear the Volkswagen any more. Must have stopped or gone over a rise.

He walked quietly and easily down the trail and then up a little grade. At the top, he moved a little to one side and took a second look. He could see the white and the chrome, now, in the first rays of the sun. He slipped into the woods and started a wide circle that would bring him close to the car. When he got close enough, he saw that it was empty. He continued on parallel to the trail, moving softly and quickly from tree to tree, always keeping an eye on the trail and watching for the kid. He had come into a pine forest, now. The ground was blanketed with fallen needles. A squirrel chattered at him, and Lucas stopped dead behind a tree.

After a minute or two, he eased his head out, just enough so he could see. Lester was standing in a little clearing just down the slope where another trail joined. Lucas pulled back, scarcely breathing.

He looked all around him now, taking stock. There were shafts of sunlight in the tops of the tall pines. He listened to the silence. Gradually the sounds of the woods came to him—a rustling of a bird in the bushes, a limb scraping, and a crow calling way over the hill.

Lucas eased his head out for another look. He heard her before he saw her. And then, here she came down the other trail in her blue and white jogging outfit, blonde hair bobbing along on top of her head. She waved to Lester and he waved back, and then she ran right into his arms, and man, those bodies came together!

Lucas drew back behind his tree. God Almighty, and the funeral was only yesterday! He eased out again and pulled back fast. That Gloria had the kid right by the crotch and he had his hand underneath her sweatshirt.

Next time he looked they were heading up the trail. He had his arm around her shoulder, and she had hers around his waist.

Lucas could see now that Lester had a thermos in his other hand, just like the one back in his truck. He followed them at a distance, and they turned off and went up the hill a ways to a large rock. Gloria had evidently been there before because she went around behind the rock and came back with a little bundle. In what, Lucas thought, was a very housewifely fashion, she spread a blanket out on the pine needles, and then produced another that she spread on top. She even turned the top blanket down a little. Lucas edged around so he could get a good clear view. He told himself this was part of his job, and that made him feel a little better.

They were having a little coffee now, or maybe something else. She took the cup and drank a little, then gave it back to Lester. Lucas could see his hand shaking a little even from where he was. He spilled a little of the stuff. Then Lucas just stared, open mouthed.

That Gloria whipped off the sweatshirt, and she didn't have a thing on underneath. There were the two big rosebuds. Then she pulls off the pants and stands there for a minute, naked as a jaybird with only little panties on. She leans over and kisses Lester and then gets between the blankets. Lester takes off his glasses, puts them to one side, slips out of his pants, and gets under the blanket with her.

Lucas didn't know what to think. He looked down at his own hands. They were big, calloused, and a couple of fingernails had dirt underneath. He took out his jackknife and cleaned the dirt out. Wait 'til he told McPhee. Then the thought struck him. He sure as hell could never tell Martha!

He looked out again, and they were just having at it. She was on top and that old blonde hair was a-bobbing away. Well, he was supposed to watch. Part of the job.

Next time he looked, they were having some more coffee and Lester was lighting a cigarette for her. His hand was shaking worse than ever. No wonder he was nervous on the job. That's what put McPhee onto him in the first place. Lucas wondered if that Gloria had put him up to the murder? A fellow could get to the point where he'd do most anything for a woman like that. He had eased down, now, and sat with his back against the tree. He sure couldn't tell Martha. He thought of his boys, and the football game Friday night. That young one wasn't too bright, but he sure could carry the mail. He picked at the pine needles and stuck one in his mouth. Then he eased around a little to take another look.

He stared in wonderment. God Almighty, they were doing it again. Lester was on top this time, and she had those long legs wound around him tight. He looked at his watch. Hell, it wasn't five, maybe ten minutes. Lucas just watched. Those two wouldn't see him if he came by on a motorcycle. He shook his head in disbelief.

The next time Lucas looked, she had her pants back on and was combing her hair. She sure was a handsome woman. Just stroking that hair in the morning breeze. Lester was fumbling around looking for his glasses. He found them and evidently they were broken. So what did he expect? She kissed him again and put on her sweat-shirt, rolled up the blankets, and put them in a sack. All ready for the next time.

Lucas had had enough. He got up and drifted back into the woods, keeping two big trees between them and him. He just bet young Spur had spent time between those same two blankets. No wonder the kid was shot! And now he was playing second fiddle, or was he? Hell, she looked like she could keep a whole country band going! Who could tell with a woman like that?

He waited where the trails met and Gloria and Lester hugged once more and Gloria went bouncing down the path, jogging yet. She waved to Lester and he waved back, the broken glasses in his hand. So now he goes to work. What a way to start the day!

Lucas started back through the woods and was in time to see Lester pull onto the highway, swerve to miss an oncoming truck, and head off towards the plant.

Lucas followed in the pickup. What a way to start the day! But Lucas was a little broad-minded, too. He could think of worse.

17

McPhee and the Golf Pro

McPhee had felt pretty good after his run, shave, and shower. He'd called in, and they told him the prowler had called his lawyer at seven-thirty and was now back in his cell, sleeping. Nellis was to call the garage about the cycle. McPhee had decided to stop by the Emerald Valley Golf Course.

He was sitting on the bench outside the pro shop. He had a little coffee in a paper cup that came out of a machine over near the door. It was still early, and the grass was wet, and he watched an older lady in a miniskirt hitting a ball on the putting green. She'd hit it to one little flag, pick it out of the cup, and then hit it to another. Every time she hit the ball it left a little track in the wet grass. Pretty soon she picked up the ball and started back towards the pro shop. She had to go right past him.

McPhee smiled as she approached. "Kinda wet out there?"

"Yes, but I love to play early. I'm an early morning person. I've already played nine holes. Putting was way off, you know."

McPhee didn't know, but he was getting tired of waiting. "What time does Mr. Desmond usually get down here?" He waved at the pro shop.

The old lady looked at her watch, and McPhee looked at her arm. It was brown, real brown, and wrinkled from the sun. Her face was the same way.

"You mean Wally? Oh, anywhere between eight-thirty and nine. He doesn't have regular hours. We just sign the sheet and go play." She indicated a little stand by the door, with a pad attached to it.

McPhee said, "Thank you, ma'am."

He watched her put the club in the bag on the back of the pull-cart and tramp off to what he guessed was the tenth tee. When she got there, she planted the ball on the little tee, took aim, and whacked that ball a county mile!

Good legs, he thought, trim, athletic-looking body. The ball sailed down the fairway and out of sight. He tried to think of his mother hitting a ball like that. His mother with her jellies and jams and church suppers, cooking over a wood stove. It was a different world. He wondered if the woman had any kids.

He got up and walked over to look at the pad. Its stand had a little roof over it to keep out the rain. He couldn't read the signatures. There were only three. He checked his watch. Eight-fifteen. A fellow came walking down the path with a towel around his neck and a mug of coffee.

"Mornin', Mr. Desmond?"

"Wally, Wally Desmond. I'm the pro here." He smiled and offered his hand.

"McPhee, Sheriff McPhee." He shook the fellow's hand and waited until he unlocked the door.

"Wally, I'm just checkin' around a little. Everybody sign that thing before they go out to play?"

"They're supposed to. It's a way of knowing who's out there. We get calls, you know, and it helps us, too."

"Do you keep the sheets after they sign?"

"Sure do, to tally 'em up. We know, then, how many use the course, when the play is heavy, and so on."

"You got the sheet for last Sunday?"

"Yeah, in the shop."

Wally opened the door and McPhee followed him in. He snapped on the lights and went over to a file cabinet back of the counter. He came back with a folder, leafed through the sheets, and then pulled a few out.

"Sunday, big day, what time about on Sunday?"

"Just let me see 'em all, if you don't mind."

"Well, they should be all in order, you know, from the beginning of the day to the end. Always heaviest play in the morning, specially on Sunday. There you are."

McPhee glanced at the date at the top of all the sheets. It was the right date. Then he looked at the times.

"They start early, don't they?" He saw one at seven-fifteen, then another. He looked carefully at the signatures. Then he went through the rest, stopping here and there.

"That's why we put the sheet out front. They just sign and go early in the morning. Can I help you?"

"No, it's okay. We're just checkin' a little. One of those domestics, you know, husband and wife stuff."

Wally nodded. McPhee didn't know whether he believed him or not and didn't much care.

"You ever play, Sheriff?"

McPhee shook his head. "Don't have the time. I have to work for a living. How long does it take to play?"

"Well, this is a regular championship course, well over six thousand yards, but in a cart maybe three, four hours. Now, some walk and that would be more, but it depends on how many are on the course, how fast the play is."

McPhee nodded and handed him back the sheets and watched him put them back in the file. "That elderly woman in the miniskirt. She sure can hit the ball. She must have driven that ball two hundred yards."

"Ah, Mrs. Thatcher, we call her 'the queen.' She's good. Plays every day. I'll tell you something else. She has two or three vodkas and she plays just as good. Remarkable woman."

"Well, thanks. We appreciate it."

"Any time, Sheriff, any time."

Back in his car, McPhee took his notebook out of the glove compartment, and placing it on the steering wheel, he wrote: "Bradham, starting time, 7:20; Thatcher, starting time, 7:30."

18

Second Team Meeting

IT WAS ABOUT ten when McPhee showed up at the office. The place was empty except for Simmons in the dispatcher's cubbyhole. He stuck his head out. "Nellis left a note."

McPhee took the note. "Mrs. Watson around?"

"She called. Dentist appointment."

McPhee walked back to the cells with the note in his hand. The prowler was asleep on the bunk. One pant leg was slit, revealing the bandage on the man's calf. McPhee thought about rousting him out, thought better of it, and looked down at the note in his hand.

"Booked him. Called the garage to get the cycle. He called his lawyer at seven-thirty, Atlanta, 841-1785."

The phone number had a familiar ring to it. He went back to his office and sat down. Reaching into his back pocket, he took out his wallet and the card from Maria. The numbers were the same.

He leaned forward and put his elbows on his desk. Came close to making a name for yourself, McPhee. Scratch one F.B.I. agent. Then he sat there wondering if the agent was really after what he thought he was after. Maybe he should call Maria. He decided against that. He was sitting there staring at the blotter when Lucas rapped on the door. He had told Lucas he wanted a meeting Thursday just as soon as Billy got back.

"Billy's back. He just went for coffee." He came in and sat down. "Had a little somethin' goin' on out to your place."

McPhee passed it off. "Prowler, who knows?"

"Heard you shot him."

"Just nicked him in the leg."

"And that Nellis. I guess he let that fella come right over the rise onto his bumper before he turned on his lights."

McPhee nodded. He might have killed him, but you can't argue with success. "How'd you make out, Lucas?"

Lucas shook his head. "That was really somethin' else, that Lester."

"And Gloria?"

"How'd you know?"

"Well, I didn't for sure. But I knew she went jogging. With house guests and a husband around, I just thought she might be doing a little something more than running through the woods."

Billy showed up at the door holding a coffee. He came in and shook McPhee's hand. "Hi, Sheriff."

"Have a good trip?"

"Yeah, yeah. We had a great time, Sheriff, a great time. I put those statements right there on your desk. Signed and notarized. And look at that typing, no mistakes at all. They got stenographers down there."

McPhee picked up one of the statements. "I know, Billy, you told me."

"They got stenographers?" This from Lucas.

"Sure. They go first class down there. How you been, Lucas?" You'd think he'd been gone for a month.

"Wait 'til you hear." He nodded at McPhee, who was reading the report. "Wait 'til he gets done."

McPhee, still reading, handed the other statement to Lucas. "Here, Lucas, take and look, and close the door, Billy."

Billy shut the door, sat down, and sipped his coffee. "Prowler out to your house, eh?"

McPhee answered while he was reading. "Yeah. We got him."

Billy went on. "One statement is from the fellow I met on the river by the name of Zybarski, and the other is from the fellow that was waiting in the pickup. They took turns. Sounds a little fishy, but maybe it's okay. You got the other fella's." He said this to Lucas, but Lucas was reading.

McPhee had finished. "They're both the same?"

"Almost word for word. Just the one guy saw the canoe and all, but according to the other guy, that's what he told him, too."

Lucas put the statement back on the desk. "Sounds like he got there just a little too late. Maybe five minutes earlier and we would have had an eyewitness."

McPhee leafed through the report with the ends of his fingers. "Whoever it was, he was too smart for that. He probably waited at the "put in" long enough so that he knew no one was right behind Jaynes. That way he could not only have been sure he left, sure he was without a helmet, but also sure no one would come down on him. Evidently his timing was a little off."

Lucas and Billy looked at one another.

Billy spoke up. "Lochmiller?"

"Could be. Could be Lochmiller hired these guys, and they made the story up just to cover." He cocked his head to one side.

"I don't know, Sheriff. I thought it sounded pretty good, but you never know."

Lucas was getting fidgety. "You want to hear what happened to me?"

They both looked at him. McPhee settled back. "Sure, Lucas, what have you got?"

"Well, I got to this Lester's house about a quarter to six this mornin'. I parked my truck about a half a block up the street."

Lucas then took them step-by-step through the entire episode. He described how Lester and Gloria met and what they did. When he used the word "crotch" he fully demonstrated the action on himself. Then he told how they went back up the hill. How she had the blankets stashed behind the rock, through the first interlude, and then the second, including the broken glasses. Then he stopped.

There was silence in the office as they all thought about what he had seen. Lucas was shaking his head.

Billy looked very serious. "Lucas?"

"Yeah?"

"You sure they didn't do it a third time?"

That broke them up, and McPhee had to grin. He thought, however, that now was a good time to lay it all out to them.

"Now what we've got here, fellows, is somebody that's a real sharp operator. It was a beautiful chance to make it look like an accident and get away with it. Whoever it was had to know almost exactly when he left. They knew he left early, so the chance of someone else being around was pretty slim. They probably waited to make certain no one else followed too closely. They had already made sure that the helmet wasn't in the back of the truck, but they probably double-checked that as well. Are you with me?"

They both nodded. They were listening.

"Then they, or he or she or an accomplice went down and waited below the sluice. They had to know where it was and that it was the most dangerous spot on the river. When Jaynes came over, they called and beckoned to him. He put the front of the canoe on the beach, took a couple of steps inside, holding onto the gunwales the way an expert would. Then he stepped out and reached down to pull up the canoe. When he reached down, the murderer hit him in the back of the head. A little blood got on the canoe, but not enough for the murderer to see it there. It was just getting light. At high water it takes forty minutes from where Jaynes was put in to get to the sluice.

"Then the murderer held him under and drowned him, and floated his body out with the current. The pouch with the money and ticket must have come out of his pocket sometime when the body was in that pool. Then, according to what Billy suspected and what this fellow saw," he indicated the statement on his desk, "he floated the canoe out after the body and then used the bucket to wash away his tracks. Now, Billy figured a good deal of this out the other day, but that's the way I think it happened, too."

Billy spoke up. "These guys could have had a contract on him. Atlanta is a tough town, you know?"

Lucas spoke up. "Mostly they shoot people. These guys, at least one of them had to be able to run that river."

Billy came back. "They could have just put a ticket in the box and then drove down, put the canoe in below the sluice."

Lucas looked at him. "Why put it in at all, then?"

They were quiet again. McPhee had gone all through this himself the other night, but it helped to hear it from someone else.

Lucas went on. "If they were hired, somebody had to show 'em where to go and they had to be around to get the word that it was all set. I don't know. After seeing Gloria today, I think she could have done it on her own."

Billy came back. "She went jogging Sunday."

McPhee broke in, "And Jaynes has got two trucks. She could have handled the helmet and taken the other truck over to the sluice herself. Unless somebody helped her."

He thought of Spur and that look of pure hate in his eyes. "We've got to get to Spur again. Jack him up, if need be, until he talks."

Billy asked, "Bradham played golf that morning?"

"He signed the sheet for 7:20. The pro doesn't come on 'til after eight. I checked this morning."

This went on for another hour. They went back and forth until each of them understood all the movements that had to be accounted for, all the items that had to be checked, including a bucket somewhere, and all the people who may or may not have seen something. McPhee was pleased. They sounded like professionals. Each had an assignment.

Billy was to talk to Mrs. Bradham and ask her about that Sunday morning, and contact Curtis in Atlanta for anything else he might get on Zybarski. Lucas was to find Spur and bring him in if he wouldn't talk, and then talk to Lester. McPhee was to check further on Lochmiller's actions in Atlanta. He didn't say how he was going to do this, but he hoped Maria would be able to tell him tonight. And he was also to see Gloria.

When they were all done, McPhee sat back in his chair and put his hands behind his head. "You know, fellas, there's one course of action we haven't thought about."

They looked at him expectantly.

"We could call Asheville and have them send a team down from the state."

Billy and Lucas stared at him.

He went on, "Up until now, everybody thinks it was an accident. We can't sit on this thing for very long without them coming in anyway. They'll be here, mark my words. People like Lochmiller and Contel only like to deal with the top men."

Lucas was indignant. "In Bryson County, we're the top. This is our case. I thought we were doing great. What could they do that we can't do?"

Billy came on strong, too. "We figured how it was done. And I think we've got it narrowed down pretty well." He indicated the notes on McPhee's desk. "What do they want, the F.B.I.?"

McPhee winced. They'd might never forgive him if they found out. He also knew that what he said was true. The state people would be all over them since they were dealing with an outfit like Contel, and it would be hard to hold them off.

McPhee pulled his chair up to his desk. "All right. Suppose we do it this way. We don't tell anybody what we've got. We sit on this whole thing at least through Monday. Your wife doesn't know what you found out, does she Billy?"

Billy shook his head.

"And neither does yours?" He looked at Lucas.

"God, no. I don't think I could tell her if I wanted to."

"So if we get any questions, we're still buying the accident, but just tying up a few loose ends, at least through Monday. That gives us four more days, not counting today. None of this is going to be easy."

They looked at McPhee. They both felt they had a stake in this case. That it was their case as well as his, even though he'd have to take the heat. Both Billy and Lucas nodded silently.

McPhee had one more visit to make before he dealt with Spur, but he didn't tell them that. And along about now, he wished he was really as confident about this whole thing as he sounded.

19

Spur's Story

McPhee came back from lunch to find Spur sitting by the counter. Lucas wasn't around anywhere.

"Hi, Spur."

"You put that up there?" He pointed at the Burger King plaque.

"No. The old sheriff left it there. I just haven't gotten around to taking it down. Want to come in?"

Spur went in and sat down. McPhee closed the door behind them. He seemed to be in considerable more control of himself than last time. McPhee didn't go behind his desk. He sat in the other visitor's chair. He wanted the whole truth, and he didn't want anything in between them.

"Lucas said you wanted to see me."

McPhee said, "I appreciate your coming in, on your own."

Neither said anything, and McPhee let the silence hang there.

"I don't know about you, Sheriff, but I think that guy was killed."

McPhee looked at his feet. "Jaynes?"

"Yeah. He was too good. He could go over that sluice

with a blindfold. He was that good. I went down with him once. We went over that sluice like it was nothin'."

At this point McPhee didn't know whether to encourage him to talk or let him go at his own pace. He decided to let him go on his own.

"He was different, though. When he talked to you, it was as if you weren't there at all. He could be talking to that desk or that window for all he cared. You know what I mean?"

McPhee nodded in agreement. He knew a lot of people like that.

"And that Lester, you ever meet him?"

"No, I never did."

"Talk about being far out. He was out of the ballpark, in a different world. Maybe he did know about computers, chips, and all that stuff, but that's all he did know. He was weird."

McPhee thought it was about time to help him out a little. "Lucas tell you what he saw?"

Spur seemed to be examining the palm of one of his hands. He was wiping the palm of one hand with a finger of the other. "Yeah, he told me. I guess that's why I came in. I liked her, Sheriff. I really did. She listened to me, and she knew what I was talking about. She was real smart, too. I thought she was real special but. . . ."

He wiped his palms on his jeans and looked out the window. McPhee thought of his wife in Raleigh. He had somc idea of what Spur was going through, and he knew it wasn't easy. He cleared his throat and shifted in the chair.

"That's why I came in. I thought I'd better clear my name, even if it meant trouble. I went looking for her that morning."

"Gloria?"

"Yeah."

"What morning was that?"

"Sunday. When Jaynes got killed. We were pretty close, you know? But then she got this thing for Lester, and she told me that maybe we shouldn't meet together so much, maybe cut it back a little. I know it was Lester, though."

"You used to go jogging with her?"

"Yeah. Well anyway, on Sunday, at first I was going down the river, so I wrote my ticket and put it in the box. Then I got thinking about Gloria. I knew she went jogging every Sunday. Foss said he'd kill me if I saw her again, but I decided to go anyway."

McPhee could understand that.

"I drove downriver, crossed the bridge, and just as I was coming around the bend, I saw her pickup, the blue one, going into that road that goes to the sluice. I swear, Sheriff, there were two people in it."

McPhee sat up and leaned forward in his chair. "You're sure about this, Spur?"

"I swear it was her pickup, the blue one, I'd know it anywhere."

"Were you close enough to see who was in it?"

"I think there was two of them. Her and Lester. Ya' see, I slowed down so they wouldn't see me, and then I got to thinkin'. So I drove over past the entrance to Emerald Valley. There's a little trail off the highway just beyond it where we used to meet. Lester's Volkswagen was there, parked in the woods."

McPhee thought about that. The Volkswagen was there and Spur did see the pickup going in the road to the sluice.

"That's why I didn't want to tell you before."

McPhee's voice was quiet. "I'm glad you told me, Spur. You did the right thing."

Spur looked at him with still some doubt in his eyes. "You think so? It's not like telling on somebody?"

McPhee looked at his shoes. "We can't let people get

away with murder, even if we care about them. Sometimes it's rough, that's all. And you had to clear your own name."

"That's what I figured."

"You tell your daddy, Spur?"

"Nobody can tell him anything. He's a smart-ass know-it-all!"

"You're his son and you owe it to him. He loves you, Spur. It's just that you scare the hell out of him."

"Me, scare him?" He raised his eyes in wonderment to McPhee.

McPhee looked at him and nodded. Then he looked down at his shoes. He felt like he was a hundred years old.

Billy called a little later. "Pete?"

"Yeah, Billy."

"I just talked to Mrs. Bradham. She's okay, Pete. She's really sorry about all this."

"What did she say about Sunday morning?"

"She said her husband took the truck and went off to play golf. He got back about ten, and then they went to the Jaynes's. She said Lochmiller was there, and Gloria came in a little after they did."

McPhee made a mental note that Gloria had plenty of time. Also, that no one really knew when Lochmiller did get back.

"You know what, Pete?"

"What's that, Billy?"

"I think she drinks too much."

"That's too bad, Billy." He hung up. This was Thursday. Another week like this one, and he might drink too.

20

The Agent's Second Visit

WHEN MCPHEE GOT home that night there was still light enough for him to see the blue Skylark parked in the driveway. She'd said she'd call. Neither she nor the dog were to be seen. He went around the side of the house to the back. There she was, sitting in the rocker, the dog beside her. Both of them looked at him as if he was an intruder. Neither made a move.

Then he looked down the pasture and up over the ridge where the sun had left a deep orange glow silhouetting the topmost trees.

"It's beautiful." She began rocking again, and the dog came to greet him. "You ever look at it?" She was still rocking.

He scratched the dog's head. "Most every night and morning."

"And when I think of what I look at every morning and night." She stopped rocking. "Pull up a chair, McPhee, and set a spell." She tried to make it sound like country.

He went over and sat on the floor of the porch near

her, but not too close. Just so they could hear one another easily. "I thought you were going to call?"

"I did, but you were out and I didn't want to make a big thing about it. So I just came on out."

"Nice to see you."

He had decided not to mention the prowler until she did. After all, it was her phone number.

"Good to be here. Want a beer?" she gestured with the one in her hand.

"Yeah, I might have one."

"There in the refrigerator, on the bottom shelf." She grinned at him.

"They teach you breaking and entering at the F.B.I. Academy?"

"Getting into your house, McPhee, is not exactly like breaking into Fort Knox. Most people do a little better than a hook and an eye."

"It's the faith, hope, and charity we have up here. It gets to you."

"I know. Like a rock in the head."

"You've heard?"

She nodded. "We keep track. This is the age of communication, remember?"

McPhee went in to get the beer. The dog followed him. He filled the dog's dish, got the beer from the lower shelf in the refrigerator, and took them both back on the porch. "Want some chips, cheese?"

She shook her head.

He set the dog's dish down, and came over and sat a little nearer her on the edge of the porch, and leaned against the post.

"So you think you got a murder?" she asked him.

"We think so."

"Who's the we?"

"Billy, Lucas, and myself, nobody else yet. We're setting on it. How did you hear?"

"One of our people got that report from the Atlanta police this morning on Zybarski, the one that saw somebody push the canoe into the river. Incidentally, I did get a man on Lochmiller, located the jet as it was coming in over Atlanta. Our man was on him when he got off the plane. He checked into the Regency, had a late dinner with some character, and slept in. I left before we got the full report. You think he might have hired it done?"

"It crossed my mind. We've got a couple more things now. There was a bloodstain on the canoe, same type as Jaynes, rare AB negative, and this local boy in town swears he saw Gloria, and possibly a boyfriend, turning in onto the road to the sluice at about the time the murder took place."

"If it was an accident, there'd be no blood on the canoe."

"Right."

"Who's this boyfriend of Gloria's?"

"Lester something. You probably know him. He's not one of yours, is he?"

"No, but we know him. Actually, he has one of the sharpest minds in the business. He's a budding genius."

"Not any more."

"What do you mean?"

"Gloria got ahold of him, jammed his circuits."

Then he told her about Lucas and how he saw them meeting in the woods. When he finished, they both sat silently. The sun was down, and the gloaming was settling in.

"Gosh, McPhee, you're in it up to your neck."

McPhee couldn't keep it to himself any longer. "Yeah, I even had a prowler last night."

She looked surprised. "A prowler?"

"Sometime after three in the morning. He was interested in the canoe." He nodded to where it set over in the shed.

"That's Jaynes's canoe?"

"Yeah. The one with the bloodstain and the hole in it."

Maria started to get up and sat back down. "Did you get him?"

"I shot him in the leg and one of my deputies ran him down on his cycle when he was trying to get away."

"Well, who was he?"

McPhee had to hand it to her. She was good. "We don't know. He wouldn't talk. But when we let him make a phone call, he called your number."

She looked at him. "My number?"

"The one you gave me to call. Said they could reach you any time of the day."

"Ah, no." She seemed genuinely distressed. "And you shot him?"

"Just in the leg, nothing serious."

She sat still in the chair, evidently putting it together. "Wainwright. Wainwright must have put him on it, and whether you believe me or not, I had nothing to do with it. As you know, McPhee, that stain is vital evidence. It changes the whole picture up here, and evidently he had to know firsthand."

"Why didn't he come and ask? Or let you find out?"

She shook her head. "You don't know Wainwright. If somebody gives him information, the first thing he does is get somebody else to check it out. That's probably why he's so good."

She began to rock again. "And you shot him? Where is he now, McPhee, in your jail?"

"Where else? I've been waiting to hear from you people all day. After all, he did call in. I figured it was your move."

"Yeah. That's right. You'll probably get a call from the Atlanta police tomorrow saying he's wanted there for bank robbery. They'll come and get him."

"You didn't know?"

She stopped rocking and looked at him openly and apologetically. "No, McPhee, I didn't know a thing. But I'm sorry. It's . . . well, it's the way things are."

McPhee believed her.

After a moment she began again. "Well, we've got two things. We've got somebody selling to the Russians, that's mine. And the murder, that's yours. And I think they can't help but be connected. As a matter of fact, since we know now it was murder, I'd say Jay Jay was killed because he found out what was going on, trans-shipping the product, or components to Russia. And whoever is doing it, killed him."

McPhee didn't reply.

"Generally, Jay Jay was straight. Oh, he was one of the bright boys, he pushed, he wheeled and dealed, but I don't think he would betray his country."

"No Benedict Arnold." The word "betray" had brought the name to mind.

"No, I don't think so, not his own people. That leaves us with Gloria, Lester, Bradham, and Lochmiller."

"Would Gloria have that kind of access to the plant?"

Maria snorted. "A woman like that has access to most anyplace. She and this Lester could handle it, and she'd have the insurance as a bonus, close to a million with double indemnity."

"And there's Bradham, he works with Lester, and I don't think he was on the golf course that morning. And old 'Locky' would have had a bonus, too, get Jay Jay off his back."

"Yeah, we've got four live suspects." She waited a moment. "You know, McPhee, you weren't scheduled to get into it this far, at all. This wasn't the way it was supposed to work."

"What does that mean?"

"You were supposed to conduct your investigation, confirm the fact that it was an accident, and close the case. My job was to keep an eye on the country sheriff and make sure he didn't blunder around and screw up what we've been working on for over a year."

"Why a whole year?"

"Knowing is one thing. Proving is another. This transshipment thing used to be a regular sieve. Industrial espionage is tough enough when it's homegrown, but when you throw in money the way the Russians do, it's murder, figuratively and literally. We're getting closer now. We put a lot of time in on this case, and I hope it's not all blown to hell."

"You want me to say that I'm sorry?"

"No. No. We'll just have to wait and see. Since they didn't make a move last weekend, maybe they'll try again soon when they think things are quieting down. It's just the way the penny drops."

It was dark. The tiny lights of the fireflies began to show down toward the pasture. They both watched, each aware of the other's seeing them. McPhee shifted a little. "You know why they light up?"

Maria knew but she said, "Tell me, McPhee."

"It helps them find one another." He was getting hungry.

Maria stopped rocking. "How about supper? I brought it."

"You brought it?"

"I wanted to be sure it was good." She leaned over and smiled in the dark. "You like lasagna? I make the best lasagna you ever tasted. I've had men after my body, McPhee, that were stopped cold in their tracks when they got as far as my lasagna."

McPhee laughed. It was the first time he'd laughed all week. "Maria, you sure know where to hit a guy."

"I'm glad you understand that. I even brought the wine, Lambrusco 1985. It's really very good. If you get the things out of the car, I'd like a shower first."

A cold wind had blown up outside, and McPhee had made a fire in the fireplace. Three logs were burning with a good, solid flame, licking up one from the other, throwing shadows about the room. One of the shadows was that of the dog, who had one foot in the lasagna pan while he diligently polished the bottom as well as all four sides. They had pillows on the floor and candles on the coffee table. The wine bottle was almost empty. Maria's pillows were against the couch. McPhee had his against his chair. Their feet were perhaps three feet apart. McPhee had recently noted this. He also noted that her toenails were painted red. She'd come barefoot from the shower with a long wraparound skirt and one of those shirts that ties around the waist.

"How'd you happen to get into the F.B.I.?"

"My daddy had three girls."

"So?"

"He thought the F.B.I. was going to save the world, even during J. Edgar Hoover's time. And he wanted a boy to carry on."

"So?"

"So mamma wasn't about to try again, and I thought it would make him very happy."

"Did it?"

"I think so. He died while I was still at the academy. He planned to have a big celebration when I graduated."

"I'm sorry."

"Who can tell? Maybe he knows I graduated. I like to think so. I was raised religious, and a little of it is always there poking around outside your garden. You understand?"

"Yes, I do." McPhee realized that it was his turn now. She had given him a bit of her private mind, those thoughts reserved for people that were close, those thoughts that let one know you were capable of loving something or someone. Loving enough to make a commitment. Enough so that you'd see it through. It just wasn't McPhee's style to talk about it very much.

"Well, I don't know. I was in the army for a while. Finished college. Sold insurance. Made a little money and came back when my daddy died."

He looked at the fire and saw one flame close to the end. It would catch and burn, then it would go out. Catch and flame up, and then out again.

"Things are different up here in the mountains. Laid back. The people that live here seem to be a little more in control of themselves. They think more slowly, on purpose, and they resent anyone who tries to do their thinking for them."

He looked over at her for a little reassurance, but she, too, was staring at the fire, maybe listening, maybe not.

"I guess I felt more at home, more sure of myself up here. There were not so many smart-ass people all trying to have a good time."

"What's wrong with having a good time?"

So she was listening after all. "Well, I just wasn't sure if they were having a good time, or if I was. It seemed that you always had to be into something, or going somewhere, having a few drinks to loosen up. I'd never felt that way when I was growing up. And the army was not much, either. I guess I just couldn't fit in down there."

He realized suddenly that she was "down there" and she didn't seem to like any of those people. "It's not that they're not good people. I guess it's just that there are such a hell of a lot of them."

"What about the sheriff's business? That's a pretty structured job, law enforcement?"

"I had to do something. I thought about insurance. Nothing wrong with it, for some people. Or maybe a small business, but I always thought the law was important, especially in this country. I guess I wanted to get into something that I thought was important, not only to me but to other people as well."

"You still think so?"

"Yeah. I guess I do. It keeps 'em from hurting one another. It's the only way. You have to have law before you have anything."

He lay there and looked at that flame again. It was still coming and going, a little weaker now. The dog had gone over and was curled up against Maria's thigh.

"You said it pretty good, McPhee."

He got up, then, and started to reach for another log.

"Leave it the way it is. I like it best when it's burned down a little."

He started back to his pillowed chair, but she patted the rug next to her and pulled another pillow off the couch. He stretched out next to her and snuggled her warm body alongside his. He rolled over a little and put his arm under her head. With his other hand, he pushed the hair away from her face and kissed her lightly on the cheek and then on her mouth. He could feel her whole body respond and come closer as she pulled him to her.

The dog got up and walked into the kitchen to get a drink. When he came back, he went over by the fire, leaving them to one another.

21

The Morning After

WHEN MCPHEE AWOKE in the morning, she was turned over on her side, away from him in the big double bed. He cautiously looked at her hair, the way it was spread out, all black and shiny, on the pillowcase. Then he looked at the curve of her hip. Somebody had once said that the curve on a woman's hip was the most beautiful thing in the world. He thought about that for a while. Neck lines and breast lines weren't so bad, either. Nor was a smile. Sometimes a woman's smile beat the hell out of most anything.

He cleared his throat and shifted in bed a little. No response. Well, maybe she was tired. It must have been pretty late when they got to bed. And even then they didn't go to sleep. God, she was strong when she wanted to be. McPhee lay there thinking how it had been.

He got out of bed and out of habit pulled on his shorts and sweatshirt. Then he went over and looked at her face. Her head rested on one arm, and the other arm was crooked up below her chin. Now this was a woman. This was a whole woman the way God did it when he was at his best. He looked at her and saw her chest rising and falling evenly. She had no gown on, and McPhee looked at what he could see of the breasts—nice, round, firm with dark nipples. He hoped she'd open her eyes, but she didn't. She looked like she might be good for another hour.

He softly padded into the kitchen, and the dog came with him. He spooned coffee into the percolator, filled it full of water, and plugged it in. He went back and looked at her again. She hadn't moved. He thought about waking her, but Jesus, she lived "down there." This was probably good for her. Needed the rest.

He went back into the kitchen, and the dog was waiting. He whined a little, and McPhee put his finger to his lips and let him out. The dog bounded out the door and off the porch. About ten feet off the porch, he turned and sat. He also started to quiver a little. McPhee nodded and held out a placating hand. "Okay, okay," he said under his breath and sat down to pull on the tennis shoes. He gave an extra tug to his sweatshirt, and they were both off the mark, heading for the creek at the end of the pasture.

The fog lay in long, low layers over the creek. When they got to the crossing, McPhee reached down with cupped hands and splashed the water over his head and on his face. He was coming alive again, now, and he felt good. The dog watched him from the opposite bank. McPhee could have sworn he had a grin on his face. He started up the path on the other side of the creek into the woods. The dog had disappeared, as usual.

Humming to himself and starting to sweat, he made the turn onto the log crossing the creek and slowed down a little. Halfway across he felt his foot catch, and then he was far out and high over the pools and rocks below. He seemed to be floating through the air, and the trees and sky were tipped all sideways. And then he hit.

When he opened his eyes, he could see the rock. It was right in front of his eyes and it was wet. His cheek lay against the wet rock. He could hear the water, and then he could feel it on his legs. He tried to move his head but nothing happened. So he closed his eyes again and listened to the water.

Something was poking at his shoulder now. It was a heavy poking, and he wanted to tell somebody to leave him alone. He opened his eyes again, and this time he saw the man. He'd seen him somewhere but he couldn't remember. The man had a fence post and he was shoving the end of it at McPhee's body, poking at his back, now his hips. He was pushing at him with the post, and in the distance a dog was barking.

McPhee felt his body move a little, and then a little more as the man pushed at his body from the shore. Then he felt the side of his face starting to slip down the rock. He could see the figure clearly now, pushing at him with the pole.

McPhee found a little crevice with his fingers right close to his face, and he dug in his fingernails and held on. He tried to move his legs but nothing happened. The pole came down on his fingers now, and his face. Again and again. Then he slipped all the way in, and the water was cool on his head. He felt the pole again in the middle of his back. It was holding him down and he couldn't breathe.

Maria opened her eyelids slowly and looked at the mountains. It was a square little window with a wooden sash, the kind that slid up and down. A shade, a regular old tan window shade, covered half of it, with lace curtains on each side. McPhee's house. She turned her head and saw the empty bed beside her. She took in a long, deep breath and let it out in a big sigh. Then she stretched way out flat on the bed and looked out the window again.

Coffee would be nice. She called, not wanting to start the day yet. "McPhee?"

She listened and heard something drop on the tin roof

and thought how the rain would sound in a big storm. She pulled the covers up around her neck. "McPhee."

She listened to the silence again. This time she heard it, the coffee pot. It was perking, and then it stopped. Must be done. "McPhee, you out there?" Louder this time.

She swung her feet off the bed and pushed back her hair. Reaching over to her bag, she found a sweater and pulled it over her head. She then wrapped the skirt around her and went to the back door while still fastening it. She opened the door and hollered again. "McPhee, you hear me?"

She listened and thought she heard a dog.

She went into the bathroom, brushed her hair, and came back out. The dog was barking again down by the creek, barking a loud, sharp, persistent bark. The coffee was done. The red light showed at the bottom. He must have been gone . . . she looked at the kitchen clock, ten to eight. He was out jogging. She waited a moment for him to come jogging out of the woods, down there where the dog was barking, and reassure her. But he didn't come.

She knew then that it was wrong. Something was all wrong, and she ran into the bedroom and pulled on a pair of tennis shoes and started out the door. She stopped, ran back, rummaged through her bag, and came up with a .38 special. Then she went tearing out the door.

When she got to the woods, she saw where the path emerged from the creek. She ran in full stride right up to the log across the river. She saw the dog, first, down in the ravine. McPhee lay in the water, and a man was holding him under with a fence post in the middle of his back. When the man saw her, he dropped the post and started scrambling up the bank. She spread her feet and screamed at him, "Stop, or I'll shoot!" She had the gun in both hands and she had him in the sights.

He kept scrambling, and she eased the strength into her finger on the trigger and shot. The gun jerked up, and she took a breath, held it, eased it out, and shot again. She saw him jerk and begin to slide backwards down the bank.

Holding the gun out and away from herself in one hand, she started slipping and sliding down the bank to McPhee.

Farney was sitting at his kitchen table reading his bible before he went into work. His lips silently formed the words, and his finger moved slowly across the page and then dropped back to begin the next line. The sound came to him again and he stopped. With his finger still holding the place, he raised his eyes a fraction and looked at a spot on the oilcloth just beyond the book and listened. It was the same as last time yesterday. He glanced up at the clock. Seven twenty-five. Same time, too.

He went back to the book and started reading again. He liked to finish his scripture before he went into work. The sound of the motor was coming nearer now, slowly as it climbed the grade. His finger stopped moving and he cocked his head. It grew a little louder as it came closer, passing by his drive down the hill from the house. This was the third morning he'd heard it. He couldn't see the road from the house, but he looked out the window in that direction. Still misty outside.

Nobody lived up the road. It just went on a little way and stopped. Just over the ridge from McPhee's place. Nothing up there but an old apple orchard, the creek, and the mountains.

He heard the truck make the turn, and then the sound gradually faded out. He couldn't tell if it stopped or faded out. No, there it was again. He listened hard, but then it was gone.

Three days in a row, now. Seven twenty-five. Deer came through that old orchard many a time. Maybe some old boy looking to get himself a little out-of-season meat on the table. Or maybe he had a trout hole. Couple of good ones up a ways.

He was alone in the house. No wife, no dog, no nothing. He sat there listening to the quiet; the light shining over his shoulder, his finger still on the place, and his mouth open a little to dampen the sound of his own breathing. The refrigerator motor went off. A squirrel dropped on the tin roof, pattered across, and stopped.

Three days in a row. He didn't know how long the truck stayed up there. He'd not thought much about it before. Just went on into work. He tried to picture the fella leaning against a tree trunk, rifle slung under one arm. If he really wanted a deer, he would have made it into the woods before daybreak.

He slowly closed the book in front of him and reached for his red John Deere tractor hat. His hand stopped midway. There was another sound, now. A dog barking. Could be McPhee's dog. It was a different kind of barking, though. Not like he'd treed a squirrel or a coon. More like he was at bay.

Farney put on his hat and got up, all in one motion. He walked easily and purposefully to the corner by the kitchen door. He took a handful of buckshot from a basket on the shelf and slipped them in the pocket of his overalls and, with his other hand, he picked up the shotgun. He went out the door, closed it quietly behind him, and started down towards the driveway, opening the shotgun, putting a shell in each barrel, and snapping it shut. He didn't run, but he moved fast in long, easy strides.

He came to the truck, a little blue Toyota, and saw it was empty, but the dog was still barking, closer now, down by the creek. Moving through the woods, he eased down the slope. The brush was getting thicker, and he had to take care with the gun, holding it high out of the way. He heard somebody holler, and then there were two shots. Farney slipped the safety off the gun and broke into a trot. At the edge of the brush, he stopped and peered through the branches.

A woman with a handgun was coming down the opposite bank. A man was laying in the creek. Farney stepped out of the bushes, put the gun to his shoulder and both barrels on the woman.

"Hold it!"

The woman saw him, saw the gun, and froze.

Farney said loud and clear, "Drop that gun."

She took a second look at the double barrels and dropped the gun.

Farney eased the gun from his shoulder and came down into the creek as if it wasn't there. "Now back off."

Maria backed off. Somehow she knew that the man would blow her away with both barrels if she didn't. She pushed the fear down and out of her gut and forced the words out of her mouth.

"That's McPhee, the sheriff, and he's drowned. He needs help and he's hurt badly. There's a man up on the bank," she motioned with her head. "I shot him."

Farney stared at her. He looked down at McPhee, then turned briefly until his eyes found the man on the bank.

Maria started foward slowly. "I know what to do. I can help him, please." Something in her voice touched him.

He recognized McPhee, took another look at the man on the bank, and then the dog. The dog had stopped barking.

Farney moved back three steps. Then he motioned her foward with the gun. He watched as she slowly turned McPhee over in the water, eased him half out, and gently turned his head to breathe life into him. When he saw the wetness around her eyes, he eased up the bank to the other fellow and poked at him with the muzzle of his gun, still keeping an eye on Maria.

When he came back, she said, "He's breathing."

Farney held the shotgun in one hand now, muzzle down. "Who are you?"

"I'm a friend of his, an F.B.I. agent."

Farney looked down at the girl. Then for some reason he started looking all around at the trees and woods on all sides as if he expected to see a few crouching men in dark suits with guns.

He looked back down at the girl. "That other fellow is shot pretty good but he's alive. Where's the phone in McPhee's house?"

"Next to the bed."

Farney swallowed. "I'll call right away." He started up the bank, quickly and without effort, but he stopped to pick up the handgun. As he slipped it in his pocket he turned and looked back. "I'll stay to tell 'em where to go."

Billy got into work early that morning. He'd slept like a log in his own bed last night, and Julie had even brought him coffee to wake him up. He parked his car and noted with satisfaction by the clock in the dashboard that it was only seven forty-five. He liked to be the first one in. He waved to one of the fellows in the tax collector's department and went up to the office.

Simmons met him at the door. He was white, really shook. "There's been a shooting over at McPhee's place and he's hurt bad! Call just came in. Can't get the fellow on the road. Must've stopped for coffee, and I'm all alone!"

Billy's head shifted gears, and he grabbed Simmons by the arm. "You sure? McPhee's?"

"Call just came in. I was—"

"Get the ambulance down there first. Then get two backups for me. Two. Then get Lucas down there, right?" He was holding Simmons with both hands, now. "The ambulance, two backups, and Lucas, right? Get Nellis if you have to. He lives out that way. Got it?"

"Got it." Simmons ran back to his cubbyhole, and Billy took the steps down two at a time.

With the lights and siren, he wove his way carefully around the square and down towards the highway. When he hit the highway, he went flat out to eighty-five.

Billy was worried. He knew there were a lot of people around that wanted McPhee to fold under pressure and be done with it. Lot of them thought he was nothing but a green, college-educated smart-ass. People were funny, sometimes, in these mountains. If they got something in their craw, sometimes they couldn't just spit it out.

He swung around a big eighteen-wheeler like it was glued to the road.

And these big shots with their money and defense contracts. He'd heard the talk about spies and the Russians, and he knew that all that barbed wire and the cameras and guards weren't for teenage vandals and petty thieves. There were some big, black clouds and lightning in this one, and he was afraid one of those clouds had opened up and come down to strike McPhee. You just didn't stand out there against people like McKusick and Lochmiller and Contel and Gloria without something coming from somewhere and knocking you down. Billy knew that for sure.

He eased on the brakes and swung off onto McPhee's road. He had to cut it back to about fifty with all the curves and hills. You don't help nobody if you don't get there. The thought helped him settle a little as he pulled into McPhee's drive.

An old man with a shotgun was standing in the driveway.

Billy skidded to a stop. "Who are you?"

"Name's Farney. Live just over the ridge. Ambulance comin'?"

"Yeah."

"They're down by the creek. Sheriff and another fellow gut-shot." He pointed the way with the shotgun. 'I'll tell the ambulance where to go."

Billy took off around the edge of the field on an old tractor trail. As he got out of the car he could hear the wail of the ambulance out on the highway.

A woman's voice called out to him. "Down here."

She was a nice enough looking lady, and she was sort of curled up around McPhee's head.

"How is he?" Billy went down on one knee.

"He's breathing."

It sounded more like a rattle to him.

"Who are you?"

"Maria Orsini. I'm an F.B.I. agent."

Billy looked at her. She said it like she meant it.

"That man up there," she nodded to point the direction, "was trying to drown him and I shot him."

Billy got up, looked at McPhee, then climbed up the hill to where the other man was lying on his side. He'd slipped down the hill and started to roll over, but a small tree stopped him. Both hands were holding his belly. There was an intermittent rise and fall to the man's chest. Billy thought he knew the man. His face was smeared with dirt, but he thought he'd seen him before.

He leaned down and patted the pockets for a wallet. Found it, pulled it out, and flipped it open. A Visa card—"Joseph R. Bradham."

The sound of the ambulance was close, now. It must be coming down through the field. He slipped the wallet into his pocket, went down past McPhee and the girl, and out to the edge of the field. Showed them where to back it in. A cruiser was following the ambulance down, and Lucas was out of the car almost before he stopped. "They get him?"

"I don't know. He's still alive."

Billy pointed the way for the paramedics.

"What happened?"

"I don't know that, either. That girl down there says she's an F.B.I. agent and she shot that other fellow up on the bank there. It's Bradham."

They watched as McPhee was brought up on a stretcher, Maria following along. She had a blanket wrapped around her.

Billy asked the medic, "How is he?"

"Not good, but he's makin' it so far."

When they brought up Bradham, Billy went over and gave the medic his wallet. "Maybe something in there to help. But no comments to anyone on his I.D. Understand?"

The medic said, "Right," and put it in his pocket. "Relatives?"

Billy said, "Yeah, okay on relatives. Nobody else, and on McPhee too."

They closed the doors and drove away.

Maria said she wanted to sit down, and Billy led her over to the cruiser and opened the door.

Lucas said, "You ain't goin' to faint, are you?"

Maria gave him a look and said, "No, I ain't goin' to faint." She sat sideways on the car seat, her feet on the ground.

She told them about McPhee going jogging. And the dog barking and how she came with the gun, and how the man had a fence post in the middle of McPhee's back, was pushing his body under, and how she shot him. They asked if she was working on the Jaynes case and she said the F.B.I. was interested. Nellis pulled up in his cruiser, and Farney was in the front seat with his shotgun. Farney got out and went over to where they were standing. He pulled the revolver from his pocket and gave it to her.

"I had no way of knowin', ma'am."

Maria looked up at the deep-lined, weather-worn face beneath the John Deere hat. "I understand, Mr. Farney. You did the right thing and you were a big help. Thank you."

Farney touched the red hat. "Thank you, ma'am." He took out a pocket watch and looked at it. "I'd better be gettin' along. I'm a little late as it is."

Billy said, "Thank you, Mr. Farney. Before you go you might want to give us your statement."

Billy didn't mean it to, but it came out sort of formal-like, and it caught the old man off guard. He looked at Billy, then at Maria, then back at Billy, and tilted his hat back.

"I ain't got nothin' to say. Just glad I could help."

Billy put a hand on his shoulder. "We just want to know what happened." He motioned Nellis over.

"Just heard the truck and came on over, is all I done."

Nellis took him over to his car, leaned on the hood, and took out a notebook.

Lucas had moved back towards the creek. He called out, "Billy, can I see you a minute?"

When he came over, Lucas was picking at his ear with his little finger.

"Who's the girl?"

"You heard her. She said she was an F.B.I. agent."

"You believe that?"

"Yeah. I guess so."

"McPhee never said nothin' about any F.B.I. agent nor any girl."

"Maybe she just came on the case. They got women."

Lucas was quick to pick him up. "I know that. I just haven't seen one before. It's queer, that's all."

Billy looked back at Maria sitting in the car and Nellis and Farney leaning on the hood.

Lucas continued. "You're still in charge. It's our case, right?"

Billy pulled a blade of grass and stuck it in his mouth. "Yeah, I guess so."

"Whatcha goin' to do?" Lucas had a knack of getting right to the point.

"We better call in Asheville," Billy answered.

"Asheville!"

"Just for the technical people, y'know. Get them all down here. You might stay here and look around a little yourself." He looked up and saw another cruiser making its way down the field.

Lucas was worried. "What about them TV people and all that? I hate them people. Can't we set up a roadblock or something?"

"That's good, Lucas. You do that out on the highway. Tell 'em we've had an accident out here. Nobody gets in—no press, no visitors, nobody."

"What about the girl?"

"I'll take her up to the house."

"Right." Things were shaping up, now. Somebody was in charge. Lucas went over to meet the cruiser, and Billy went back to Maria.

"Feeling okay?"

She wiped some of the hair out of her eyes and handed Billy the pistol. "I guess."

The cruiser was heading back to the highway, and Lucas and another deputy were going back to the creek.

"Want to go up to the house and get cleaned up?" Billy asked. "Maybe a little coffee?"

Her hair and face were smeared with mud, her eyes were tired-looking, and she was wet, soaking wet.

"Yeah, I better call Wainwright." She lifted her legs into the car and Billy shut the door. He was walking around in front when Lucas suddenly came charging out of the woods. Billy stopped, his hand on the door.

Lucas slowed to a walk, and when he got to the car he rested his hand on the hood. "Just like I figured, Billy. He used a trip wire. Put a loop of fish line on that old tree that crosses the creek. Nailed it on both sides. When McPhee came joggin' across it, it pitched him right off on the rocks. Never had a chance. Then he went to pushin' him under with that post. Drown him, y'know."

Billy looked at him and then down at the door handle. "Just one more accident, eh?"

"You got it. One more accident and the heat is off. Real dirty way to get a man."

Billy looked up at him. "Two men, Lucas. Two men."

At the hospital Billy and Maria had to wait. Finally a doctor had come out and asked if they were relatives. Billy said, "No." The doctor said he had no authority to give out any information to anyone but relatives. Billy thought about that for a bit. Then he recognized his own order not to give out information and he was very pleased. He explained to the doctor how McPhee had no relatives, around here anyway, and he had been the one to give the order. He showed his credentials. The doctor had looked at them and then at him. Billy could tell he wasn't used to taking orders from Indians. Finally, the doctor sat down and told them.

McPhee had a broken hip, and they were getting a man in from Ashville. He also had a ruptured spleen, and they had sewed that up. Loss of blood and internal bleeding. Billy wasn't sure where his spleen was, but he nodded as if he knew that was the right thing to do. And lastly, a concussion, and there was considerable pressure but there was nothing to do but wait and see. They might have to operate.

Billy knew about concussions, and he nodded again, saying the word "pressure."

Maria asked if they could see him. The doctor said they were moving him, and anyway he was still unconscious.

Maria asked about Bradham.

The doctor told them the bullet had passed all the way through the body and missed the spinal column. There had been considerable loss of blood, and infection was always a problem in stomach wounds. They had repaired the damage but couldn't be sure about the infection until later. Both were presently listed as "critical."

He asked if he could release information he had given them to the media people.

Billy said, "Yes."

Maria said, "No."

Billy explained that he could release the information on McPhee, but not on Bradham.

Maria showed her F.B.I. card and you could tell the doctor felt better about the F.B.I. than he did about Indians.

Billy helped Maria check into a motel and went back to the office. He didn't ask her anything, and she didn't offer anything. It was delicate. No newspaper or TV people there, and that was a relief. He pictured the roadblock and the complaining and thought that was a good move. He told Mrs. Watson and Simmons about McPhee and went into McPhee's office and closed the door. He didn't feel he was taking over, he just needed a place to be alone and think and make a couple of private calls. He also wanted to see McPhee's notes.

First, Billy called the judge. He had to repeat his name. "Billy Birdsong, Judge. I'm Chief Deputy."

"Ah, sure Billy, what is it?"

Billy explained the whole thing. Couple of times Billy stopped to ask if he was still there, and the judge grunted. When he was done, he asked if he should carry on as usual, even though McPhee was out of it temporarily.

There was a silence at the other end.

"Did you hear me, Judge? I asked if I should carry on as usual since McPhee is temporarily out of order?"

Billy was sorry as soon as he said it. It made the sheriff sound like a telephone, but the judge didn't seem to mind.

"How long did the doctor say he'd be out of it?"

"He said he didn't know. Maybe twenty-four hours."

It was only a little lie, but Billy didn't want them to lose the case to the state people. McPhee wouldn't want that.

"You say you've already gotten their technical people on the attack on McPhee?"

"Yes, sir."

"And there's an F.B.I. agent involved. What are they doing here?"

"I don't know but I'll ask," Billy said.

"Well, I can't see what difference twenty-four hours will make. Can you handle it?"

"Sure, Judge, no problem." He lied again.

"All right, Billy. It's in our jurisdiction, and for the next twenty-four hours you're acting sheriff. You're in charge. Just keep me posted."

"Thank you, Judge." Billy hung up and let out a long sigh.

Billy knew he had a day or two, at most, and then he'd be up to his ears with Asheville or the F.B.I., or both. He was wrong. The phone rang and it was a fellow by the name of Wainwright with the F.B.I. in Atlanta. Wainwright was concerned, but he said he'd heard a lot of good things about Billy.

Billy figured he was being nice, but said "Thank you."

The only thing that bothered Billy was that the man called him "Birdsong." He had never been called "Birdsong" before by anyone.

The man continued. "This fellow Bradham, uh, Birdsong, why do you think he tried to kill McPhee?"

"I'm not sure. I guess he thought McPhee was closing in on him on the Jaynes murder."

There was a silence on the other end.

"What do you mean by that? Maria Orsini called me this morning and said Bradham had an alibi. Signed in and played golf that morning."

"Well, maybe, but we don't know for sure."

"Oh? Let's see here."

Billy guessed he was checking some notes.

"Yes, I see what you mean. Well, uh, Birdsong?"

"Yes, sir."

"You don't think Bradham moved against McPhee because McPhee found something wrong at the plant?"

"I don't know. McPhee never said anything about the plant. But then he never told us the F.B.I. was in on it either."

"Yes, I know. But it's my understanding your department is still handling the case and you're in charge?"

"Yes, sir."

"Well, we're very interested as you know. I'm sending a contingent up to work with you and I'm sure you'll cooperate. Right?"

"Yes, sir."

"Now there's just one more little detail. You have a man there that was shot while prowling around McPhee's house."

"Yeah. McPhee shot him in the leg."

"This man is wanted in Atlanta for bank robbery. I want him released to us, just as soon as my men get there. You'll take care of that? No problem?"

"No problem. I'll take care of it." Who makes problems with the F.B.I.?

"I knew I could count on you, Birdsong. We appreciate it."

"Yes, sir." Billy hung up.

Billy was uptight. Too much too fast. He breathed deeply and looked out the window at the mountains. It was clear, but no sun. He sat that way without moving for a full five minutes. Then he called Julie and told her he was acting sheriff, in charge of the case. She told him he'd do just fine.

Lucas came in about eleven-thirty. He didn't say anything. Just closed the door and sat down. "We still got the case?"

"Which one?"

"Both of them."

Billy nodded. "I don't know for how long."

They both looked out the window.

Lucas took out a wooden match, stuck it in his ear, and twirled it between his fingers. Then he looked at it and threw it at the wastebasket. He missed and got up and dropped it in. He looked at Billy. "This case meant a lot to McPhee."

Billy kept looking out the window. "I know. Us too."

Lucas posed a question. "Didn't Spur tell McPhee he saw a blue pickup head into Bull Sluice that Sunday morning?"

"Yeah. He thought it was Gloria's."

"There was a blue pickup parked on the other side of the creek, down at McPhee's place. I checked and it was Bradham's."

Billy picked up a paper clip and bent it out straight. "That's close, but it's not horseshoes. Close don't count."

"What do you mean?"

Billy sighed. "Bradham went after McPhee because he knew McPhee was closing in on him. Bradham knew McPhee didn't think Jaynes had an accident. We all thought he got killed. Bradham was supposed to be playing golf. So far, we sure can't prove he killed Jaynes. And we don't know why he'd want to do it, anyway. He was supposed to be a friend of Jaynes. Then there's this whole F.B.I. stuff. We don't know a thing about that."

They sat there. Inaction always got to Lucas. "What are you goin' to do next?"

Billy looked at him and their eyes met. "I think I'll go see Thatcher."

"Who's Thatcher?"

"I don't know, but that was the last thing in McPhee's notes. 'See Thatcher.' "

"I think you ought to see Gloria, too."

"Why?"

"If you'd a seen her in those woods, I swear Billy, that woman's a drivin' demon. That's what she is. Maybe they did it together."

"You think she knows something?"

"She knows plenty."

"Okay, I'll see her, too. What are you going to do?"

"I'm goin' to get Lester."

"The genius that took his pants off with Gloria in the woods?"

"Yeah."

"Goin' to bring him in?"

"No, as a matter of fact, I'm not goin' to bring him in. I'm goin' to take him out." Lucas looked grim. "Someplace where there's just me and him, and we can talk."

Billy was concerned. He'd seen Lucas mad one time when a young buck had spit in Lucas's face. Lucas knocked him down and swore he was goin' to jerk the young buck's arm out of its socket and throw it up in a tree. He had his foot planted on the guy's shoulder and was about to give the arm a wrench when Billy got him from behind and he came out of it.

Billy spoke slowly. "No rough stuff. McPhee wouldn't stand for it, and it could foul up the whole case."

Lucas shook his head. "I know better than that. I'm just goin' to explain to him how serious this is." He looked earnestly at Billy.

"Maybe, Lucas, you should pick up Maria, and then both of you could bring him back here. She's down at the Vista Motel, and maybe you can find out what was going on down at the plant."

Lucas squinted at him. "Well, maybe so. But I'll talk to him some alone first."

Billy settled for this. "Yeah. Okay, Lucas."

Lucas got up and left, and Billy reached for the phone.

22

The Way It Was

"WELL, WHO IS SHE?" Billy tapped a pencil on McPhee's desk and shifted the phone to hear better.

"She's just an old girl that likes to play golf. She's good, too."

"Did McPhee ask about her?"

"Yes, as a matter of fact he did."

Billy was talking to the golf pro. "Where does she live?"

"Well, I . . . I'm not supposed to give out information over the phone."

"I won't tell anybody," said Billy, and he meant it.

"Here we are, Barbara Ann Thatcher, 610 Fox Run Drive. That's in the community."

"I know," said Billy, "and thanks. Thank you very much!"

Number 610 was a brick house with white columns in front. It didn't look as if anyone lived in it, but the lawn and flowers were all very nicely trimmed. Billy rang the doorbell, and a dog started barking. Not a real bark, sort of a cross between a sneeze and a cough. Billy figured it was a small dog.

A tall, elderly lady in a blouse and shorts opened the door. She didn't peek out or anything. She just opened the door. Had the dog in her arms.

"Mrs. Thatcher?"

"Yes."

"I'm Billy Birdsong with the county sheriff's office. I'd like to talk to you."

"What about?"

"About Mr. Bradham, Joe Bradham."

Billy saw the change. Her eyes dropped, and she seemed to hold the dog closer.

"You do know him?"

"Of course." This was a quieter voice.

"Can I come in?"

She opened the door wide and closed it behind him. Then she led him into a room crowded with furniture, overstuffed furniture. The arms and legs on everything were curved and all highly polished. She switched off the game show on the TV and motioned him to a chair. She sat in a rocker next to a table. There were three pictures on the table, and a half-filled glass. She still held the dog, and she began to rock him like a baby.

"Another one of your men was out to see me yesterday."

"Sheriff McPhee?"

"Yes, I think that was his name."

"What did he want to see you about?"

"Well, why don't you ask him?"

"I can't Mrs. Thatcher. He's been in an accident."

"Oh, I'm sorry to hear that."

She stopped rocking and put the dog on the floor. The dog sat and looked at Billy.

"Well, he asked me about golf. If I played early in the morning."

"Do you?"

"Yes. Herbert and I always played. I lost my husband two years ago, but I'd become accustomed to playing and I like the game, so I play most every morning."

"What else did he ask you, ma'am?"

"He asked if I had played last Sunday."

Billy waited.

She seemed to be sensing what was coming, and she reached down and put her hand on the dog. "I told him, 'Yes, I had.' Then he asked if I had seen Mr. Bradham on the course. I told him that he had signed the sheet on the line just above mine. There's no one there, you see, at that time of the morning, so we just sign."

"What time was this, ma'am?"

"About seven-thirty."

"Well, did you see Mr. Bradham?"

"No, but I know he was there. He was the only one that signed ahead of me, so it had to be him."

"What do you mean?"

"Well, when you play early in the morning the dew is still on the greens. You can see where the ball has rolled and where people have walked. It makes the greens very slow."

"So you saw his tracks on the green?"

"Yes. I knew he was there. It makes one feel a little less alone."

She was looking at the design in the carpet, now, and telling the story to herself.

"But that was what was odd. Because after the third hole, there were no tracks. None at all on the fourth green or any others." She spread her hands in front of her and shook her head. "No more."

"And this is what you told Sheriff McPhee?"

She looked up at him. "That's right."

Billy sat there looking at her. "Did the sheriff say anything after that?"

"He said I was not to tell anyone what I'd told him." She reached down and picked up the dog and began rocking again.

"And did you?"

"Well, you see I have known Joe Bradham for a long

time, many years. I have played golf with him any number of times, and he and Herbert played a great deal together. Mr. Bradham is an executive with Contel, so I thought I owed him at least that much."

"Did you tell him, Mrs. Thatcher?" Billy's voice was flat.

Righteous tears had welled up in her eyes, but she spoke softly. "Yes, I did."

Billy got up from the couch. He looked at Mrs. Thatcher, and he felt just plain damn sorry, but he was afraid of what he might say to this poor old lady with her TV and her dog and her glass and her golf.

He murmured, "Thank you," and as he went out the door he heard her voice.

"And he was a charter member of the club."

Billy drove around through the development and up the mountain to the house with the great deck, the Jaynes's house. When he rang the bell, a maid came to the door and told him that Mrs. Jaynes was at the club, so he went to the club.

He always felt a little uncomfortable in a place like this. Like he didn't belong. Like it was a different world. Today was no exception. He pulled open the heavy cedar door that said Members Only and walked in. He stopped inside the door. It was dark, and it took time for his eyes to adjust. He thought somebody might come and ask him if he was a member, or maybe to go around to the side door. Then he remembered the uniform and that he was "acting sheriff." Julie had said that.

He took a deep breath and walked over to the bar. The bartender came over and stood in front of him, across the bar. Billy said the name. "Mrs. Gloria Jaynes?"

The bartender stood there looking at him. Then he nodded out towards what looked like an enclosed porch. He even leaned over a little and pointed.

Billy thanked him and went out on the porch. Mrs.

Jaynes was sitting there smoking a cigarette with a drink in front of her. He was afraid of this woman, but he didn't know why. He guessed maybe it was the sex business he knew about, and because she was real attractive. Big and strong, too.

"Mrs. Jaynes?"

She turned her head, and all that fancy hair turned with it. "Yes?" The eyes had that same faraway look he'd seen the last time, but he wasn't sure about the focus. Even when she looked at him now, it was as if she looked through to the back of his head, rather than his face.

"I have to talk to you. Can I sit down?"

She moved the head a little as if it was okay, so Billy sat down. He hitched up his chair. "You do know young Spurgeon Foss, right?"

Her eyes came into full focus on him for a moment, and then she looked out at the golf course. "Yes, I know Spur."

"He says you were with a Lester Rennbarger last Sunday morning, the day your husband was murdered."

"Murdered?" She looked at him again with a little curiosity.

"Yes, murdered. We know for sure it wasn't an accident. Were you with Lester when your husband was killed?"

"Yes, as a matter of fact, I was with Lester."

"Where did you go?"

"We went jogging, Sheriff, jogging together on a mountain trail near the community."

"Will you sign a statement to that effect?"

She thought about this for a while and eased the ashes off the end of her cigarette into the tray. "To that effect, yes, I will."

So far, so good.

"Is that all, Sheriff?"

"No." It came out too quickly, but Billy went on.

"McPhee was hurt badly this morning. We think Mr. Bradham tried to kill him."

"Why would he want to do that?"

"We think he did it because McPhee figured Bradham killed your husband, and he was closing in on Bradham. Bradham felt the investigation would stop if McPhee was out of the way, and people would go on thinking it was an accident."

She was still playing with the cigarette in the ashtray. "I guess you can think what you like."

"Do you know why Bradham would want to murder Mr. Jaynes?"

She was back with that faraway look in her eyes again. She sighed, and a faint smile seemed to ghost across her face. She turned and looked out on the golf course. When she spoke it was as if he wasn't there. "If you can't soar with the eagles, they always want you to quack with the ducks."

Billy said nothing.

Gloria turned to him. "Tell me, Sheriff, I understand Joe Bradham was shot. Is he going to live?"

"Yes, I think so."

"And you want me to tell you why Bradham may have killed Jay Jay?"

"Right, Mrs. Jaynes. We need a motive. Can you help us?"

"Of course I can help you. But if you think I will, you're mad."

Billy shriveled.

"You see, I've known Joe Bradham for a long time. He could actually do only two things well. Golf was one, and the other escapes me. But the poor man had absolutely no balls at all. More recently, I think he discovered this, and he tried to get out of the circle. He had no idea what it was like, and he made mistakes. But if he's not dead, I'm not going to help kill him."

She took a long drink, then, and looked at the green,

where another foursome was approaching. He decided she'd had a few but was holding them well, so far.

She looked back at Billy and gave him a faint, condescending smile. "That's all I can tell you. I do hope it helps."

Billy thought about the eagles and the ducks, the balls and the circles, and he started to get up. He didn't respect this woman, but she was treating him like dirt. He thought of her up in the pines screwing her brains out with Lester, and it made things easier for him. He didn't know how to ask the question, but he knew he had to have an answer. Finally, it just came busting out. "How do you know he had no balls, Mrs. Jaynes? Were you ever a friend of his, too?"

She looked at him a little surprised and raised her eyebrows. Billy felt her knee touch his. She smiled at him now, an easy smile, and this time the look in her eyes wasn't faraway at all. She moved up in her chair, and Billy felt a slight pressure of her thigh on his.

"You're an Indian, aren't you?"

Billy held steady. "Yes, ma'am. Cherokee."

"Oh, a Cherokee. They lived around here at one time, didn't they, Mr. . . . ?"

"Birdsong, ma'am. Billy Birdsong." He could smell her warm, spicy perfume.

"Birdsong, Billy Birdsong. What a beautiful name."

She took another drink, and it dribbled a little. This helped him as she dabbed away.

"Well, Mr. Birdsong, when I used the term, I was speaking figuratively. Let me explain so we both can understand." She seemed to be looking at his shoulder where his shirt was a little tight. "Since you're an Indian, let me put it this way."

The condescension was still in her voice, and Billy wondered if he should tell her that his grandfather was sent to prep school in England, but then he didn't see why he should.

"When the Indians went whooping around in a circle on their horses . . . around the white men and their wagons, some rode out of the circle and came closer than others, and shot more white men than the others did. Those were the ones with balls, Mr. Birdsong."

"What's that got to do with Mr. Bradham?"

"Well, when the Indians got home and stretched out between the blankets, they always told their women what they'd done."

She was having fun with him now, telling him a story, and the drinks were taking over. Billy didn't smile. He just looked at her. The thigh pulled away a little. She sat up in the chair and crushed the cigarette in the ashtray. She put her hand on his arm. Billy didn't move.

"Joe Bradham lived in Jay Jay's shadow all his life," Gloria said. "Jay Jay got the power and glory forever, amen. Bradham sang in the choir and passed the collection plate. One day," she paused here as if making a private decision, "something happened to Joe Bradham, and he thought he could be the great man. Have an office on the top floor, London, Paris, Tokyo, and Rome, the finest of cars, and godlike power, with a big, beautiful woman on his arm and in his bed. All this instead of Rotary, golf, and a lush for a wife. But he needed money, a lot of money. So he rode out of the circle."

She stopped. It was like one side of the tape had run out. But then nobody changed the tape. A little smoke curled up from the cigarette in the ashtray and drifted towards the window. Finally, Billy slid his arm out from under her hand.

For the second time that morning he felt like throwing up, but sat back a little and looked at her. He knew the name of the big, beautiful woman on Bradham's arm and in his bed. He also knew she knew that he did.

She returned his look with ice in her eyes. "I'm going to have another drink, and if you don't mind, Sheriff, I'm going to have it alone."

Billy got up and left. The bartender nodded as he went out the door.

Two TV trucks and a group of reporters were waiting for Billy when he pulled into the parking lot at the county building. He didn't look at them, and he didn't listen to the questions. He took the mike from the girl and looked at the camera, just like McPhee had done.

"At seven forty-five this morning we had a call from Sheriff McPhee's place. We found the sheriff had suffered a bad accident and another man had been shot. Both men are in critical condition, and we're withholding the name of the other man until relatives can be notified. We have received technical help from the state police at Asheville, and we're working hard on the case. Just as soon as we have more information, we'll get it to you."

He handed back the mike, but another girl pushed a second mike in front of him. "Who reported the accident?"

"Mr. Farney, a neighbor."

"Is this case related to the Jaynes accident? Is it true that the F.B.I. is involved?"

"You'll have to ask the F.B.I. about that. Thank you very much, and when more information is available, we'll give it to you just as fast as we can. Thank you."

He turned and went in the building. He wasn't sure what he said, but he remembered McPhee saying "thank you" and the more information part, so he had used it. He guessed it was okay.

The door to McPhee's office was shut. Mrs. Watson was typing, and she stopped and took a little coffee when she saw Billy. "Lucas and the F.B.I. woman and that Lester Rennbarger are in there," she said.

He looked at her. "How's McPhee?"

"No change. I called about an hour ago."

"The other one?"

"They've taken him off the critical list."

"How long they been in there?" He motioned towards the office.

Mrs. Watson drank some more coffee and shook her head. Then she began typing. "About two hours."

Billy went in. Nobody was sitting in McPhee's chair, so he went around behind the desk and sat down. No one spoke. Lester's tie was off, and he had it rolled up in one hand. He held his glasses in the other, and Billy noted that one side was missing a lens. He looked like a condemned man hoping for word from the governor.

Lucas got up and went over and put his hand on Lester's shoulder. It was a firm and friendly hand, and Billy saw a tremor go through Lester's entire, thin body. It was like watching a bull with his front foot on a puppy. "Lester wants to help us, Billy."

"Oh?" Billy looked at him. Lester stuffed the rolled necktie in his pocket and stared at the floor.

"He wants us to know he had nothing to do with Jaynes's murder, right Lester?"

Lester nodded, two, three times.

Maria looked at Billy and nodded in the direction of Lucas. "What about Miranda on this thing?"

Lucas gave her a flat-out stare. "I told him about his rights plus a little more. Ain't that so, Lester?"

He squeezed Lester's shoulder, and Lester winced and nodded at the same time.

Billy got up. "Maybe we ought to go outside for a minute. How about some coffee, Lester?"

"Yes, please."

Billy went to the door, spoke to Mrs. Watson, and held the door while Maria and Lucas walked out into the hall. There just wasn't any other place to go.

"What's it all about?" He looked at Maria, then at Lucas.

Lucas shifted a little. "I told him we had a witness that

saw a blue truck goin' into Bull Sluice about the time of the murder. The witness said it was Gloria's truck and that Lester and Gloria were in it."

"What did he say?"

"He said it wasn't him. He said he went jogging with Gloria that mornin'."

Billy nodded. "I talked to Gloria and that's what she said, too."

Lucas went on. "Well, anyway, that sort of loosened him up. We didn't tell him that Bradham had a blue truck like Gloria's."

Maria picked it up here. "Lester said that Bradham came to him about six months ago and told him he needed help. Said he'd pay Lester very well for a little evening overtime. Lester wouldn't give us a figure for his overtime, but it was probably in the thousands, rather than time and a half.

"They ship computers from here to Europe, all models, all legal and aboveboard. Primarily to their other plants and offices in West Germany. What Bradham did was to have Lester take some experimental and highly classified components and systems and incorporate them into the regular models that were signed, sealed, and ready to go overseas. Lester said there are six all ready to ship, right now. Two of the six have new components. One has some stuff from the Stealth bomber program, and the other has controlling microprocessors used in particle beam research. Part of the Star Wars program. Contel has millions in defense contracts in both these projects. For just what was in this shipment alone, the Russians would probably pay close to five hundred thousand, maybe more. If our people, or the customs agents, didn't know exactly what to look for, the chances are they'd never find it. Bradham had a broker in Germany, a KGB man who would then transship the two models with the secret systems and components to Rumania and

Russia. We knew they were getting the stuff, but we didn't know how."

Billy looked at her. "Jaynes found out?"

Maria nodded her head. "Right. Lester told us Jaynes showed up Friday, right after Lester had finished and was on his way out. Lester heard Jaynes tell Bradham off and told him he was going to turn him in. Bradham pleaded with him, said he'd clean up his act, do anything. Said they were old friends, all that stuff."

Billy said, "So?"

Maria shrugged. "So Jaynes said he would think about it over the weekend."

Lucas shook his head. "Of all the sorry-ass, dumb things I ever heard."

Billy asked, "Will he testify?"

"He was afraid we'd connect him with the murder, so he wants to make a deal. He wants us to believe that he was just following orders. That Bradham told him it was just to get the components to our overseas plants, and he said he believed him."

Maria went on. "He's willing to testify against Bradham if we help him get off the hook."

Lucas moved in. "I already told him personally that other charge would be dropped."

Maria looked at him sharply. "What other charge?"

"Public fornication on government property. That's a national forest, and if he don't know it, he should have."

They both looked at him. First with disdain, then with wonderment.

Billy leaned back against the wall and looked down at the polished terrazzo. A deputy was coming down the hall, and he waited until the man went by before he spoke. "McPhee was closing in on Bradham. He found out that Bradham wasn't on the golf course when Jaynes was killed." He told them about Mrs. Thatcher and how she had called Bradham. "So Bradham thought that if

McPhee was out of the way, it still could go down as an accident and he'd be home free."

Lucas asked, "How did he get to the sluice?"

"He had his truck parked by the third green. I checked it out. Left it there before he started playing golf."

"What about his wife? Don't she know when he comes and goes?"

"She drinks, Lucas. Heavy. And they partied Saturday night. He probably took the helmet out of the truck during the party and brought it back next morning in a paper bag."

She tilted her head to one side. "I'll have to talk to Wainwright and see what he has to say about all this, but it looks like you fellows and McPhee have got your murderer."

Lucas wiped his hands on his pants. "We got him strung up like a hog at butcherin' time."

Maria looked down the empty hallway. "I guess Bradham just saw a chance to make it big on his own. He went after McPhee, and McPhee wouldn't let go. He probably thought he could bully the small-town boys into accepting two accidents in a row. But it was just Bradham. Lochmiller and Gloria Jaynes had nothing to do with it."

Billy swallowed. He thought of that leg pressing on his, and the perfume, and he wondered. Billy felt a little sad.

No one said anything. They just started drifting back down the hall to the office and Lester.

It was almost seven when Billy finally left the office that evening and headed for home. He thought about last Sunday morning when it all began. It seemed like months ago, but actually it was less than a week. He remembered finding the body, visiting the house with the big deck, and he and McPhee going back and figuring out just how it happened. A thought struck him, and his curiosity got the better of him. He swung off the main street and headed down the highway to Emerald Valley.

As he drove past the house, he saw there were no lights. He turned around in a cul-de-sac at the end of the street and came slowly back. As he swung into the driveway, the lights of his cruiser picked up the name and number—"Bradham, 624."

The double-garage door was open, and he shut off his lights. No need to disturb the neighbors. Taking his flashlight off the seat next to him, he quietly opened the door and got out, leaving the door open. Going into the garage, he flicked the light around, first one side, then the other. It was neat and orderly—riding mower, golf clubs, workbench, tools, washer and dryer—and there it was sitting on the floor next to the dryer, a large galvanized bucket! Billy switched off his light and went home.

23

McPhee Closes the Case

THE CALL CAME about seven-thirty next morning while Billy was in the shower. Julie said she'd give him the message. The bathroom was filled with steam, and the water was making a lot of noise. She hollered from the other side of the curtain. "Billy, it was the hospital."

She could hear him singing to himself. "Billy, the hospital called."

He opened the curtain a little and got her wet. Then he shut off the water and stuck his head out.

"McPhee is conscious and the pressure is down," Julie spoke again. "They said to tell you."

Lucas was waiting for Billy just inside the hospital entrance. Hospitals were not Billy's thing, and he was glad to see him. Lucas picked up a big pot of yellow marigolds and looked nervously around to see if anybody was watching. "Martha made me bring 'em. What room is he in?"

"Two ten." Billy had a magazine and some oranges.

The nurse at the desk on the second floor showed them to McPhee's room. She was pretty and polite, and Billy was glad McPhee had a nice nurse like that.

McPhee's eyes were closed when they came in. They set down the flowers, the fruit, and the magazine. McPhee opened one eye. "What took you so long?"

Billy shrugged. "We been waitin' on you." There were two bottles with tubes hanging, one on each side of the bed, and a bandage all around his head. "How you feelin'?"

"Okay, I guess."

Lucas thought he should hold up his end. "Nice room you got here."

"Yeah. Great." McPhee opened both eyes.

Billy went on. "Everything's fine with the case."

McPhee said, "Let's hear it."

Billy asked, "Can you handle it?"

McPhee looked at him. "Sure, my head's okay. Tell me."

They told him then, in little bits and pieces, about the trip wire, Bradham, Maria, the blue truck, and even the bucket. Also, about Mrs. Thatcher and Lester. McPhee grunted as they went along, to let them know he was listening. When they were done, they just sat there. The sun was coming in the window, and it was quiet. Lucas was bent forward, his elbows on his knees, looking at the floor. Billy sat with his hands folded in front of him looking at McPhee, whose eyes were closed again. He spoke without opening them. "We got a case, then?"

Billy answered, "Yeah. I talked to the judge. He thinks we made our case."

McPhee opened his eyes. "How's the dog?"

"He's fine. He's over at my place. Julie's takin' care of him."

They didn't know it but McPhee wanted to ask about Maria. He wanted to know if she was all right, if she had stayed around, and if she was coming to see him, but he didn't know how to put it.

There was a little tap on the door. Billy saw her

standing outside. As if he were reading McPhee's mind, he said, "She's here, Pete. We better go." They shook his hand and filed out.

Maria came in, kissed him gently on the cheek, and took his hand. "How you feeling, Sheriff?"

"I'm okay."

There was a nice, warm silence.

McPhee turned his head on the pillow so he could see her next to him. "Well, we've got our case. What about you? You going to get your man, too?"

She tilted her head and grinned at him. "I'm not sure, McPhee, but I'm working on it!"

She squeezed his hand.

McPhee smiled, even though it hurt.

If you have enjoyed this book and would like to receive details of other Walker mystery titles, please write to: